A SHARED HISTORY

Black Victorians - Book 1

by

S. N. CLAYTON

Dear kai,

I hope you enjoy my first book!

Thankyou.

All the best, Sonji

S·N· Clayton

Conscious Dreams
PUBLISHING

A Shared History
Black Victorians: Book 1

Copyright © 2024: S. N. Clayton

Published by Conscious Dreams Publishing

www.consciousdreamspublishing.com

Cover Designed by: Etsy Seller: Castles & Classics
Editor: Marg Gilks, Scripta Word Services
Proofreader: Rhoda Molife, Molah Media
Typeset and ebook formatting by: Amit Dey

ISBN: 978-1-915522-83-2

Dedication

Giving thanks to The Most High for blessing me with the irresistible urge to always follow my creative passions. Nothing ventured, nothing gained!

To my mother, Joyce Clayton - thank you for teaching me to read and write before I started school. You were the one who inspired my love for books and reading, taking me to the library every week for as long as I can remember. I have this passion for reading and writing that was nurtured by your own love for literature.

May you rest in eternal peace.

Contents

Author's Note

Thank you for reading *A Shared History, Black Victorians Book 1*, the first book in my Black Victorians Trilogy.

I would appreciate it if you could help other readers find the book by providing a review and telling others about it. Please also sign up to my email list here:

www.snclayton.com.

I have always been an avid reader of Black history, and during the lockdown of the COVID19 pandemic of 2020 - 2021, I delved a little further into the Georgian and Victorian period of British history from the perspective of the black presence. Books such as *Staying Power: The History of Black People in Britain*, *Black Americans in Victorian Britain*, and *Black Jacks: African American Seamen in the Age of Sail* captivated me. My research inspired me to focus on the Black elite of Africa and the diaspora and showcase the wonderful stories of triumph over adversity. These realities tend to receive less attention in mainstream media and books on the black experience during those periods.

Most major abolitionist movements in America, the Caribbean, and indeed Britain were historically led by Black and mixed-race people with support from their allies of many colours. They were determined to create their own themes of rebellion and survival within a very complex system of slaves, free Blacks and indentured servants from various racial backgrounds. It is also interesting to see how Black and mixed-race people were legally categorised back then and how they viewed themselves as individuals and as a group. I have chosen to reflect this authentically within this book series.

My fellow black historical romance writers are my inspiration. These include award-winning author Beverly Jenkins, the queen of African American historical romance, who creates main and supporting characters from a range of races and class levels within the African diaspora. I also read the captivating works of best-selling author Alyssa Cole, which focus on the Civil War era and the integral part African Americans and their allies played in this. I aspire to join the small group of authors who contribute to the historical black romance genre, as readers of this long-standing, burgeoning sub-genre are hungry for more stories.

Prologue: 1985

Audrey Howard fiddled with the knob on the car radio. She had just finished singing along to Chaka Khan's 'I Feel for You' and wanted to listen to some rare grooves and lovers' rock on a pirate station that she knew played some wicked tunes. The signal was obviously too weak, as the radio crackled and buzzed the more she turned the stiff dial.

Her fiancé, Jonathan Langdon, peeped at her out of the corner of his eye, smiling with amusement as she continued to hum the Chaka Khan tune. Then he shifted his attention to parallel parking outside her aunt's house.

Giving up on the radio, Audrey studied him as he smoothly manoeuvred the car into the space. She loved watching him drive, seeing his long-fingered, olive-toned hands confidently handling the wheel, assuring her she was in safe hands. His black Ford Fiesta had been a much-desired graduation present from his parents on completing his master's degree in engineering, and he kept it shining brighter than a pair of vigorously polished army boots. Jonathan switched off the engine, pulled the key from the ignition and leaned back in his seat, looking thoughtful.

"Ready?" Audrey asked as she leaned back and peered into the tilted car mirror so she could reapply her lipstick. It was her favourite medium cocoa brown shade from Fashion Fair Cosmetics, a popular make-up brand specifically created for black women. It was expensive compared to the usual brands she used but it complimented her smooth, copper-toned skin. Richly pigmented lipsticks were scarcer than shipwrecked treasure troves.

"Do you think she'll like me?" Jonathan asked nervously, running his hands through the curls of his dark blond hair. His hazel eyes regarded her earnestly.

"I...like you, and that's all that matters." Audrey frowned and concentrated on applying the lipstick, pressing her lips together, then pouting.

Jonathan laughed as he watched her systemic pre-exit ritual. "Thanks, but I think I need just a tad more reassurance. I distinctly remember your parents calling your aunt 'too militant' when we were growing up."

Audrey rolled her eyes and cackled joyfully. Her laugh was contagious and had always reminded him of the actor Sid James in the popular *Carry On* films that they repeatedly showed on television. They continued to chuckle whilst recalling memories of her aunt lecturing her bored parents about black history and attending marches for various political causes. Audrey and Jonathan had both been fascinated and a little intimidated by her strong character and views, even as they enjoyed her regularly taking them to the ABC cinema on Turnpike Lane followed by the local Wimpy for burgers.

They had both grown up in south Tottenham, North London. Tottenham and the surrounding areas had always been multicultural. Working class, middle class, white English, Indians, black Caribbeans, Africans, Greek Cypriots, Turkish and East Indians rubbed elbows mostly amicably. Jonathan had lived in the street opposite to Audrey's. As children they had attended the same infant and junior schools and played quite safely and happily with each other and the other local children.

After their first year of secondary school, Jonathan's father, who had been overlooked for the post of deputy head at a local primary school, decided to take a PhD tenure at a university in Hartford, Connecticut. Their mothers had stayed in touch for a while, but eventually the hectic rituals of family life had taken over and they had lost touch.

On their return to England after many years, Jonathan and his family had moved to nearby Muswell Hill. Whilst on term breaks from their respective universities, Audrey and Jonathan had reconnected when they had both been dragged reluctantly to their old church by their mothers for a rare visit. Hanging out whenever they could over the years, it was within the last year when they had fallen for each other romantically.

Audrey sighed as she readjusted the car mirror and returned the lipstick to the black Italian leather bag Jonathan had bought for her on a visit to Bloomingdale's department store in New York last year. Slinging the strap over her right shoulder and across her slim torso, she said, "Just because my aunt is into black history and political causes doesn't mean she'll disapprove of our relationship. I mean, I kind of get what you mean, but I doubt she'll be problematic. Anyway, she was cool with you when we were little and you know my grandmother was mixed race, so why would you even think that?"

"I don't know, I just don't want anything to spoil what we have. And to be honest, my memories of her are quite sketchy. You know we've had quite a few negative reactions from some of our friends and families. They were fine when we were just friends, but it was so disappointing how quickly their attitudes changed once we became engaged." Jonathan frowned down at the olive fingers resting on the black steering wheel.

"Listen, bubs, that's their problem." Audrey cupped his face with one hand and gently turned it towards her to look directly into his eyes. "The most important members of our families are all that matter. Not fair-weather friends or hypocritical distant cousins whom I hardly see. They only seem to have a problem with mixed relationships when it involves a female member of the family, I notice."

They looked at each other knowingly and laughed.

"Give us a kiss," she ordered, light-heartedly affecting a Cockney accent.

He eagerly complied, softly kissing her Cupid's bow lips whilst anxiously eyeing her aunt's front door for witnesses.

"Coward." Audrey giggled and wiped away the trace of lipstick she'd left on his full lips. He grinned and checked his face in the mirror before they ventured out into the crisp air and sunshine.

Jonathan followed Audrey through the front door and along the corridor towards the back of the two-storey terraced house. They walked through the long, narrow

TV room dominated by two comfortable English garden chintz sofas and wooden furniture towards the kitchen, from which wafted the spicy aromas of cooking.

Her Aunt Beatrice, or Aunt B as everyone called her, had lived in the family home in Harringay with her British-Antiguan mother and Jamaican father until they retired to Florida. Jonathan had known Audrey's grandparents from attending church and the odd family event held at Audrey's house, yet he did not recall ever visiting their home. He took advantage of the opportunity to look curiously at all the lovingly framed family photos on the walls.

Jonathan was shocked to see a picture of himself staring moodily into the camera at Audrey's tenth birthday party. *I was probably starving,* he thought, smiling to himself. The boy Jonathan was crushed within a gathering of children of every racial and ethnic background residing in south Tottenham. A wide grin revealed Audrey's small, pearl-white teeth as she posed, knife poised above a square, white birthday cake. It was decorated with lit candles and pink and blue icing petals that rested on a table groaning with party food. Her tightly curled Afro hair was slicked back into two long black pigtails and she wore a navy blue jumpsuit with wide collars and a thick zip running down the torso. He smiled fondly at the memory.

It was a typical illustration, really, of their contrasting personalities. He had been more of the serious and laid-back type and she had been easy-going and happy-go-lucky. Their personalities had complemented each other as childhood friends and even more so as young adults, especially as he had learnt to be more outgoing as he got older, and she'd grown a little more serious about life.

"Hi, Aunt B. Look who I've brought to meet you," Audrey said to her aunt as Jonathan entered the kitchen behind her, nearly careening into her as she stopped abruptly and turned, holding out her arm as if introducing a star act.

The smell of something peppery and moreish hit his senses as he stepped into the warm kitchen with its pale pine cupboards and marbled worktops.

"Hi sweetie. Did your uncle let you in? I thought I heard voices at the door," Aunt B replied as she finished stirring the zesty West Indian soup in an enormous cast iron Dutch pot on the stove. She turned to face them, smiling.

"Yeah, he said to tell you that he was popping out and would be back later."

"*Yeah?* No, not 'yeah.' It's 'yes.' How many times do I have to tell you to use the Queen's English, Audrey, especially at your age? I hope that's not how you speak to the children in that junior school of yours." Aunt B rolled her eyes to heaven and kissed her teeth.

"Oh Auntie, stop it. You're so extra sometimes. You know I switch it up when I'm at work. That's the way it goes with my generation." Audrey was a trainee teacher in a junior school. Aunt B had been a secondary school teacher for years, her specialist subject was English language, and she was a stickler for speaking correctly with both her students—who had loved her—and her niece.

Jonathan smiled shyly and held out his hand. "Hi, Aunt B, do you remember me?"

"Of course, Jonathan. Can I have a hug?" Aunt B held out slim, well-toned arms and Jonathan stepped hesitantly into them, relieved by her warm welcome. All his doubts about her approval vanished with that one gesture.

"It's lovely to see you again after all these years."

"Same here, Aunt B." He stepped out of the comfort of her arms as she leaned back to look up into his face, examining him keenly.

"I detect a faint American twang in your voice now, but you haven't changed much facially. I don't think I would recognise you if I saw you on the street, though; you were such a skinny little thing. Now you're all tall, athletic, and handsome. I can see why my niece has fallen for you." She chuckled knowingly, dark eyes twinkling, and winked at Audrey.

"Aunt B, behave yourself," Audrey admonished, not looking at all surprised by her aunt's cheeky compliment.

Jonathan laughed and struggled not to blush at the compliment, but Audrey and Aunt B giggled as they watched his face redden.

Aunt B examined her niece next, and following Aunt B's lead, Jonathan paid more attention to the cerise jumpsuit Audrey wore. The colour looked great on her. And a wide black belt pulled tight around her waist accentuated her curvy hips.

"Have you got our little surprise, Aunt B?" Audrey asked, glancing at Jonathan mischievously.

"Yes, I certainly have. Let's go and sit at the dining room table."

They followed her out into the TV room and settled at the long teak dining room table set against the wall. Aunt B paused at a tall China cabinet jam-packed with ornate glasses, vases, plates and cup sets, and lifted a rustic, wooden storage box that had been sitting on the floor beside it. She brought the box with her and set it on the table. Engravings and metal studs decorated what looked like cherry wood.

Jonathan gazed at Aunt B and Audrey, pulling his eyebrows together in curiosity and smiling at their secretive exchange of glances. "What surprise?" he asked. "What are you lovely ladies up to?"

"Flattery will get you everywhere," Audrey replied, fluttering her eyelashes and flipping a coil of blue-black

xviii | S. N. CLAYTON

hair over her shoulder, the action making the large pink and black triangles dangling from her ears swing. But her eyes were on her aunt as she took a couple of black leatherbound books carefully out of the wooden box. The books were slightly dog-eared, the leather scratched. They looked as if they had been handcrafted.

"Be very careful with how you handle these. They're precious to all of us," Aunt B said mysteriously, and handed the two books and some pictures to Audrey.

Puzzled, Jonathan watched Audrey open the first book to handwritten pages. The ink was slightly faded, but still readable. The handwriting flowed beautifully across the paper.

"Jonathan, these are the journals of my great-great-grandmother, Celia. They've been carefully preserved and passed down to family caretakers for generations, preserving her perspective on our family history." She stroked the soft leather of the other journal fondly.

"I've been researching our ancestry and I discovered that our families shared a significant history," Aunt B said. "Your ancestor, Edward Langdon Sr., and Celia's father, Thomas Robertson, became close friends during the 19th century."

"Wow! Did you discover this from the journals?" Jonathan asked, eyes wide with surprise. Placing an arm affectionately around Audrey, he peered more closely at the journals.

"I have suspected the connection for years. Something seemed familiar about your family name and background, but I never had time to read the journals properly until the last couple of years. My curiosity was piqued when you two reconnected. An old university friend of mine who's a genealogist and family historian pointed me in the right direction and that's when we discovered the family connection."

Aunt B rose. "How about I dish out some soup and tell you the story?"

"Do you need any help?" Jonathan asked as she walked towards the kitchen.

"No, m'dear." Aunt B affected a West Indian accent, something that happened when she was excited. "You stay right where you are. It won't take long. Oh, come to think of it, do you two mind setting the table for me, please?"

"'Course not," Audrey and Jonathan chimed simultaneously. They all chuckled at their timing.

"You know what they say about couples, once they've been around each other for a long time, eh?" Aunt B joked, then laughed at their blank expressions. "Okay. I'll save that for another time."

The journals had been replaced carefully in their wooden box. Once they were all settled around the table with bowls of spicy soup embellished with succulent chicken pieces, boiled dumplings, and yellow yam, Aunt B told them of their ancestry. She spoke with great reverence and almost as if she had written the journal of her ancestor with her own careful hand.

Chapter One

London: 1880

"No Lady Benwick, I do not see your point. I have nothing to hide," said Mr Henderson, the local curate of two churches within the parish; the churches were attended by professionals, the gentry and aristocratic families who had townhouses in the central London area of Bloomsbury.

Edwina Faintree, officially known as Lady Benwick, was not impressed with his answer. She squinted watery blue eyes up at him, an indicator of both disdain and shortsightedness. She was too vain to wear glasses. *How dare he answer so insolently,* she thought. *Who does he think he is? He's nothing but a pompous philanderer.*

Daniel Henderson had been an infamous rake when he was younger. His cold, unfeeling heart had left Cupid's arrows bent and broken. Whilst on his grand tour, he'd taken the time to think deeply about his pointless lifestyle of loose women, card playing, and hard drinking, which, contrary to public opinion, had in fact troubled him greatly for some time. Nevertheless, no one could have been more surprised than him when some type of spiritual epiphany had unexpectedly struck him during visits to churches, cathedrals, and other notable religious tourist sites in Paris, Spain, Rome, and Venice.

On his return, he had taken time to reflect and despite the scepticism of his family and polite society, he had committed to his studies in theology. On completion, he had joined the church as a curate and, due to his aristocratic connections, had no issues serving the local parishes of Bloomsbury despite his past reputation and his direct manner. It did him no favours that he certainly did not look or act like your typical curate, with his tall, athletic figure, swarthy Byronic looks and strong patrician nose, slightly crooked (a gift from his university boxing days), that added further character to his handsome face.

"What if I were to tell your esteemed parishioners that there were rumours of embezzlement in your past?" Lady Benwick retorted.

Daniel had turned his long back to her to retrieve some paperwork from his desk. He spun around on his heel faster than a whirling Dervish. In fact, he spun so fast that Lady Benwick thought he might keep spinning, such was the force of his outrage.

"Then you would be ruining not just mine but the legacy and trust of the charity's reputation. Many of the recipients rely on the church's support and donations from wealthy families. Why would you destroy that with such malicious lies?" They were both on the board of the charity set up by his predecessor to aid fallen women who had become pregnant and needed support and shelter.

Lady Benwick placed her delicate blue and white china teacup on the side table next to her chair. The weather had not warmed up sufficiently for fires to be dispensed with, and the amber and yellow flames shimmering in the fireplace behind the stained-glass fire screen had been slowly warming her chilled body. With some regret, she pulled a pair of leather gloves out of her black beaded bag. Fingerless black lace gloves already covered her age-mottled hands, but she began daintily pulling the leather gloves over her short, bony fingers.

"Nevertheless, please bear in mind that if this rape accusation is acted upon, you will live to regret it. You would be surprised how easily willing witnesses can be conjured up," Lady Benwick said. "I have found that when it comes to the lower orders, every man has his price. Or woman, as it may be." She sniffed haughtily.

Barely able to contain his frustration at this ludicrous situation, Daniel eyed her warily. "My dear lady, your precious grandson has been accused of rape. You expect me to ignore such a serious allegation? And may I remind you that it was not so long ago that your own daughter was married to a member of the so-called lower orders who saved your family from financial ruin."

"You are impertinent, Mr Henderson." Lady Benwick rose, incensed that this insolent man would dare to challenge her. He might well be from a respected aristocratic family, but as the youngest son, as far as she was aware, he barely had a penny to his name and was living in the family townhouse in Cartwright Gardens.

She gritted her teeth. "You need not remind me of my now deceased son-in-law's dubious ancestry. However, in matters of the family's reputation, needs must prevail. My only regret is my daughter being landed with an upstart husband who was as proud of his blackamoor grandmother as if she had been Queen Victoria herself."

Back in the late eighteenth century, her son-in-law's black grandmother and white grandfather, the heir of a Jamaican planter, had grown up and played together on the plantation and had secretly fallen in love once they had come of age. Yet she had refused to marry him, as he had not stuck to his promise to free all the slaves on the plantation once he inherited.

Lady Benwick had been a strong advocate for the abolition of slavery in the USA but had been scandalised when she had found out about the ancestry and illegitimacy of her Jamaican born son-in-law. He had been registered as an octoroon at his birth. Although she firmly believed in the sanctity of marriage, she was deeply conflicted and disapproving of race and class mixing, believing that eventually the pressures of society would destroy such relationships.

Lady Benwick had always advocated that family and cultural legacy should take priority over frivolous emotions. However, graciously putting her hypocrisy aside, she had allowed her daughter to marry her late son-in-law due to his vast wealth, inherited from his mulatto father and wealthy English-born white mother. A large amount of her son-in-law's fortune had been invested in the dwindling coffers of her late husband's family estate, and she was here to protect the legacy for which so many sacrifices had been made.

Daniel raised one eyebrow. "My dear Lady Benwick, blackamoor is such an old-fashioned term. These days, as far as I'm aware, the preferred term is 'coloured'."

"Indeed? Humph," she replied with another sniff of disdain.

"Would you like me to see if I can locate some smelling salts, Lady Benwick? You seem to have developed some type of sniffing fit ever since we entered into this distinctly unsavoury conversation." Daniel gave her a tight smile.

"We digress, Mr Henderson. I hope I have made my point," she said with a slight dip of her head to the side and a meaningful look. "Please ring the bell. Your man or one of your other servants may bring me my coat and see me out."

Daniel turned his back and crossed the drawing room to the French windows. He stared out at the grassy square of Cartwright Gardens. "I'm sure you are quite capable of finding your own way out."

"Well—! I've never been so insulted in all my life! You, sir, are not a gentleman," Lady Benwick spluttered, reeling in shock.

"After this conversation, you have ceased to be a lady in my eyes, *Lady* Benwick." His voice was loaded with sarcasm. Keeping his back to her, he pulled out his briarwood pipe with shaking hands and packed it with tobacco. Surprisingly, instead of one of her swiftly thrown retorts, which were sharper than a poisonous dart, all he heard was the swish of long skirts and the soft creak of the panelled mahogany door.

The comforting scent of smouldering tobacco filled the air. That and the crackle of the fire in the hearth soon calmed him down. He contemplated the charity's future and the church's reputation. Regrettably, he would now have to persuade Lady Benwick's grandson's accuser to drop the allegations, although the accuser had initially been reluctant to press charges in fear of her own reputation being publicly sullied. Nevertheless, it would have been problematic to prove rape.

He had refused to disclose a name. However, he would surmise that the ghastly Lady Benwick would be more than willing to offer the accuser some type of monetary compensation to maintain her silence. The thought of backtracking disgusted him, but he had no choice if he was to avoid a potentially negative impact on the vulnerable women who desperately needed the charity's support.

Chapter Two

Whilst the curate pondered on the dilemma presented to him by Lady Benwick, in a townhouse in Bedford Square, Celia Robertson stood behind a rectangular pine table in the basement kitchen. She vigorously employed a long-handled wooden spoon to stir the cake mixture contained within a yellow enamel mixing bowl as she made Lady Benwick's favourite chocolate cake. Woe betide the cook if the texture and flavour were not to her guardian's liking. She sighed and resisted dipping her finger into the batter; she had just tested some on a teaspoon and the flavour was perfect.

Celia paused, wiped long, slender hands on a cotton tea towel and left the cake mixture to check the beef and dumpling stew bubbling nicely in the oven on one side of the range furnace. The fragrant smell that filled the kitchen when she opened the door made her mouth water. Next, Celia checked the water in the boiler on the other side of the range's furnace compartment, which was kept burning constantly to meet the demands of the kitchen and the household.

She placed two cast iron pots on the hotplates, ready to boil the accompanying vegetables later. She recalled her American mother referring to them as Dutch ovens and her Caribbean father calling them Dutch pots, both of them correcting her in jest if she used one or the other of the terms when they were together. She smiled at the fond memory.

Returning to her cake batter, she glanced around the long, high-ceilinged kitchen and sighed, glad for some time to herself after the exhausting journey to London. She had sent Jenny down to Covent Garden to pick up some herbs, spices and other essentials, some of which were only obtainable in London. They had travelled up from Lady Benwick's country estate in Surrey a few days before, and she had not been able to send as many pantry staples as she had hoped to with the small band of servants travelling ahead of the household's arrival.

Though she was Lady Benwick's ward, Celia usually acted as housekeeper when they were in town for the season whilst the country estate's housekeeper stayed in Surrey to oversee the house staff left behind. Celia was overseeing and cooking the household meals until the agency cook she had secured started in the next two days. She had taken to wearing an unofficial uniform of plain, dark charcoal skirts with a tiny bustle and simply designed blouses with slight pleating in the front when at home, so she would be taken seriously by the agency staff.

Celia almost jumped out of her crisp white apron as she felt a pair of wiry arms encircle her waist, followed by a kiss as light as a feather that tickled her neck.

"Edward Langdon, you scoundrel!" She laughed lightly and leaned back into his embrace, placing her hands over his.

"And what is my best girl up to?" He reached out and dipped a finger into the chocolate cake batter, which prompted a playful slap from Celia.

"Stop that at once. You know your grandmother will have my guts for garters if there isn't enough batter to make the large cake she's expecting." She turned around to face him.

Edward's hands accommodated the change of position, enveloping her in a big hug as comforting and warm as a wool shawl. He nestled his head against her long brown neck. "Mmm, you smell of lemon soap."

"Thank you for such a lovely gift, but you really shouldn't," Celia said as she stroked the honey blond curls at the back of his neck.

"Whyever not?" Ed leaned back slightly to gaze down at her, and Celia's gaze sank into the hazel-flecked depths of his brown eyes before she mentally shook herself. "Celia, you're the only girl for me. Who else would I buy intimate gifts for?"

"Ed, would you please stop talk of that nature, please? You know I'm still thinking on your proposal. I fear it will not be a successful union." She looked up at him, letting her worry show, and pulled away. "It would be problematic gaining approval from your grandmother to marry someone of a different class, let alone a coloured woman."

"What utter nonsense," Ed scoffed. "Time after time, my grandmother seems to conveniently forget your upbringing and our families' shared history. Besides, what does the colour of skin matter when we have each other's love? We're not the first mixed couple in the world, Celia, and I sincerely hope we will not be the last."

Celia could not believe Ed's utter naivety, yet it was typical of his easy-going nature. *It's all very well for him to make such a statement*, she thought. *Does he not realise the difficulties inherent in our situation?* She shook her head. *She* would be the one to take the brunt of society's censure and disapproval from whites, coloureds, and everyone else disdainful of mixed couples who decided to express an opinion. Those in the social circles he moved in would be gossiping for decades. They may have accepted her as his grandmother's ward and companion, but society's upper strata certainly would not be as welcoming and accommodating if she and Edward were to seal their relationship with a marriage certificate.

Even so, he was right about the hypocrisy of his grandmother when it came to 'family traditions' and their shared history. Celia's Jamaican father, Thomas, had been an able-bodied seaman, working on merchant and privateer ships that had taken him across the world. He'd been a proud Black Jack, one of the thousands of black and mixed heritage seamen hailing from the colonies.

Living in Britain whenever he had been on leave, he had faced racial prejudice in its many different forms within society and work, some of which could be brushed off. At times though, he faced more challenging and dangerous situations involving not only disgruntled members of society but the peelers, who cared nothing about the equality of the races or male suffrage.

Generally, he had found the complex class system and the racial bias of Britain to be the lesser of many evils present across the colonies. He had found more opportunities and a wider range of contacts including white allies, British-born coloureds, Africans, Americans, West Indians and Indians who had immigrated or visited from the colonies, all brought together by common causes and interests. Thomas could both make a living and advocate for American abolitionist and male suffrage causes here in Britain rather than back in Jamaica with its more restrictive colloquial class and race prejudices. There were of course the unspoken prejudices resulting in colour bars in all walks of life, but for freeborn Black Jacks who worked and travelled the world, it was a lower price to pay to evade the fugitive slave laws of America.

Since the abolition of slavery across the colonies in 1833, it had not worked out as well for some black and mixed race people living in Britain; certainly not well enough to build a future. Many had either returned to their home countries or immigrated to places like Canada, Liberia, and Sierra Leone with hopes of a future free from the systematic prejudices which held them back.

Thomas had met Celia's mother, Augusta, on one of his ship leaves in New York. Celia's mother had been a free coloured woman born in the American South to ex-slaves freed when the son of their master, wanting nothing to do with slavery, had sold the plantation he'd inherited.

Augusta, a teacher in an orphanage for children of all races, kept bumping into Thomas at abolitionist and temperance meetings. He lectured at these meetings to earn additional income, most of which usually found its way to charities aimed at improving the conditions of coloured people in the USA and Britain, as well as his family back in Jamaica. They fell for each other and became engaged.

He was captured by the authorities whilst on a local schooner trip in the American South, a risky job he had taken to add to his financial purse between privateer trips. The Southern authorities had suspected him of being a fugitive slave or navy deserter and refused to release him until his privateer ship's captain paid a fine. His colleagues had managed to get a message to Augusta, who contacted the ship's captain. He, along with two white shipmates, vouched for Thomas and obtained his freedom.

Her parents had married on her father's release, and he sent for her once he had returned to England and made a home for them. The mother country became his home.

His experiences as a Black Jack had inspired him to start lecturing about the plight of the free coloured people with whom he had interacted. Many of them were trying to establish themselves and improve their plight in the West Indian colonies. Others were still enslaved in the American South.

Thomas had been born to a free black woman and the mulatto son of a Jamaican merchant; the relationship had been abusive and his mother had left his father on a few occasions, taking Thomas and his sister, only to be forced to return to her abusive husband when she could not earn enough to feed herself and her two children. This was another revelation that had irked the easily scandalised Lady Benwick when he had told her his story, as she believed marriage was for life, no matter the circumstances.

Haunted by the bad memories of his family back in Jamaica and the complex fugitive laws of North America, Thomas's most pragmatic choice was to settle in England. On the advice and consultation of his white ex-seaman business partner who had advocated for him when imprisoned in the South, he had invested some of his small fortune in a number of successful ventures, including a privateer ship, schooner and manufactory.

Ed released Celia and leaned nonchalantly back against the table. "My love, I know there will be difficulties, but you are certainly considered at least middle class by most of our peers within our social circles. They've known you since you were practically a babe in arms."

"That's all very well whilst we were family friends, but how will they react to our relationship now?" she cried, throwing her hands up in despair. She strode over and checked on the beef stew before returning to the neglected cake mix.

Celia's father had met Ed's father through their passionate advocacy for abolition in the Americas and their similar Jamaican backgrounds. Despite the differences in how society saw them, they had become fast friends. Ed's father, whom he had been named after, had married into Lady Benwick's family through an arranged marriage to her daughter. It had been a marriage of convenience, as Lady Benwick's family were on the brink of losing their country estate due to bad financial management.

Ed's father, who became Celia's godfather, had been referred to as an octoroon growing up, as his own father, Ed's grandfather, was mixed blood and had married the widow of a white Jamaican planter. Ed's grandfather had inherited a fortune from his white grandfather and after successfully tracking down and purchasing the freedom of a few members of his family who had been enslaved, he made sure that he supported the abolitionist movement with both time and money. He had passed this passion on to Ed's father. Although their distant African ancestry was no longer readily evident physically and they were now effectively white and living as white people, the blood of their proud ancestors ran through the veins of both Ed and his deceased father. Sadly, Ed's mother had died soon after giving birth to his younger sister, Charlotte.

Celia's and Ed's fathers had socialised together and organised lectures, raising much-needed money for the various abolitionist, male suffrage and temperance movements of their time. They had believed strongly in male suffrage and that all humans were made equal.

When her parents had died in an accident when Celia was quite young, she had become her godfather's official ward. Celia and Ed had grown up together on Ed's family estate and in the London townhouse until they had both been sent away to school. Despite being black, she had become a surrogate member of the family in a complex Victorian age. After the death of her godfather, to Celia's relief, Lady Benwick had offered to take his place as her guardian in order to protect her from unwelcome advances from unscrupulous suitors—many of whom were willing to overlook Celia's race In order to benefit from a modest inheritance from her godfather and a generous fortune from her parents' estate, which had been held in trust until her twenty-fifth birthday.

"If I marry you, there will be no turning back if we find we have made an error of judgement. I need some time alone, Ed. I cannot make a decision right now." Celia checked the time on the big kitchen clock. "Oh dear, look at the time. I need to pour this cake into a tin."

As a recently orphaned young girl, she had spent hours in the country estate kitchen with Mrs Jenkins. The cook had become very fond of the girl taken into the household and taught her how to cook many classic

British dishes and pastries. Celia had eagerly shared with the kind-hearted cook an array of spicy recipes that had been passed on to her by her Jamaican father and American mother.

That morning, they'd had Jamaican codfish fritters, poached eggs and bacon. Lady Benwick and the Langdons had a penchant for subtly spiced West Indian cooking, in particular due to their colonial backgrounds and links with colonial gentry and professionals. Lady Benwick had also spent time with her in-laws in the Caribbean and the Southern states when younger and had a particular taste for some of the traditional black Southern dishes. The latter experience in the American South had led her to disapprove strongly of slavery, inspiring her to also support the abolitionist movement along with her son-in-law.

Celia had long wanted to open some type of food establishment or possibly a boarding house for coloured and Indian seamen who were often affected adversely with the unofficial colour bar in some areas of London. However, the boarding house could become quite problematic, as for propriety's sake she would need to employ either a male manager or a married couple rather than live there herself, which would eat into her profits.

She frowned as she realised that she had been procrastinating about moving forward into independence since receiving the bulk of her inheritance three years ago. She felt as if she was still hanging onto the safety of the Langdon family's apron strings, but she had no other close family; there was just an aunt in New York and an uncle in Bristol, both of whom she corresponded with every so often. She had no real relationship with them, due to distance.

Celia and Ed turned at the light tap of footsteps on the back stairs. A moment later Jenny rushed into the kitchen. Celia had been teaching the head housemaid the role of a townhouse housekeeper with the foreseeable future in mind, and they had grown closer in the last year. Jenny had a good head on her shoulders and was decently educated due to the generosity of a wealthy elderly relative who had believed strongly that all women should be educated, after she'd suffered the effects of her own disastrous marriage.

"Goodness. What are you doing back so early?" Celia exclaimed.

"I've been out for over an hour, Miss Celia," Jenny replied, traces of an Irish accent lending a lilt to her mild Cockney one. The plump housemaid's grey-green eyes lit up on seeing Ed. "Afternoon, Master Ed..." she said, looking coyly through her eyelashes at Ed.

"Good afternoon, Jenny. Any goodies for me, and only...me?" He grinned endearingly. Ed was generally known as an outrageous flirt and had always teased the female staff of all ages. Lady Benwick disapproved, but he usually dismissed her reservations by claiming she misunderstood his humour.

Jenny giggled self-consciously and blushed. "Ooh, Master Ed. You are incorrigible. What would milady say?" She patted the flaxen bun coiled neatly at the back of her head, taking care not to displace the small black hat pinned at a rakish angle in front of it.

Ed laughed. Swiping some of the cake mix with a long, tapered finger, he adeptly side-stepped Celia and scuttled towards the door before she could swipe him with the tea towel she had whipped off her shoulder. Used to Ed's harmless joking and flirting, Celia raised her eyes to heaven before regarding Jenny's face, still flushed with excitement.

She had loved Ed for what seemed like forever, but now that the reality of the situation had hit her, she half wished that they had left their adult relationship at the flirting stage. Her procrastination over marriage reminded her of a Jamaican saying that her father and godfather used to tease Ed and her with as children, whenever they grew tired of playing with much desired toys given as gifts: "*Wanti, wanti, cyan getti, getti, nuh want it.*" In other words, "count your blessings and don't take what you have for granted." Was she toying with Ed's feelings by allowing her fears and concerns over what society would think to hold her back? She sighed deeply and slid her finger into the remnants of the cake batter.

Chapter Three

"This is utter nonsense. I've never raped anyone and never would," Ed shouted, outraged that anyone could accuse him of something so repulsive. "Who is my accuser?"

It had been one week since the household had travelled to the townhouse in Bedford Square and they were slowly settling into a routine. Ed and his grandmother were in the sitting area of her modest apartment, which also contained a bedchamber and dressing room. Lady Benwick had decided it would be best to hold such a delicate conversation in her rooms, rather than in the family sitting room or drawing room.

Sitting regally in her favourite wingchair with her hands clasped on the plain black skirt covering her lap, Lady Benwick stared up into her beloved grandson's blazing hazel eyes with a calmness she did not feel. "Mr Henderson refused to disclose her identity." She sniffed and delicately pressed a lace-rimmed handkerchief to her nose. "It's an absolute disgrace."

"Outrageous..." Ed stalked around the room, his thumbs hooked into his grey pinstriped waistcoat. He stopped abruptly. "Why did he not approach me directly?"

"I have no idea. It was after our charity committee meeting. He may have felt the timing was conducive," Lady Benwick replied.

Ed regarded her curiously. "You seem remarkably calm." Was it him or was she avoiding eye contact? That was very unlike her. He would be mortified if she actually believed the accusation.

"Yes, well, there's little point in wearing out the rug, my dear boy. It's unlikely to resolve anything, I dare say," Lady Benwick replied. "Would you kindly fetch my smelling salts? I can't seem to rid myself of these dratted sniffles."

Ed walked a few steps into the boudoir, with its ornate four-poster bed and boldly geometric half-canopy. The room smelled strongly of bergamot oil and lavender water, with a hint of ammonia from the smelling salts. He wrinkled his nose and retrieved the smelling salts from one of the side tables.

Returning to the seating area, he handed the bottle to his grandmother and took a seat opposite her, draping his arms along the chair's curved mahogany armrests. Then he leaned forward and studied her keenly. "What am I to do? If this gets out, I'll be ruined. The business, our good name..." Ed rubbed his hand across his cheek.

"I managed to persuade him to discourage the little chit, whoever she may be, from pressing charges. However, there will be a few sacrifices to be made."

"Sacrifices?" Ed repeated, puzzled.

"Yes, I've offered to pay the girl off... I'll also be making a significant donation to the new church roof fund."

Ed widened his eyes in amazed disbelief. "Grandmama, why on earth would you agree to such a commitment without discussing it with me first? You are aware that the haulage business and estate are still struggling, and our personal finances are tied up in various investments that are yet to return the dividends we've lost in previous years?"

Lady Benwick took in the sudden change in his usually amicable, relaxed expression; now his face was pinched with concern and anger. She prayed that what she was about to say would bring him to his senses in relation to the family's future. His father was partly responsible for the financial difficulties that they found themselves in, as he had made some questionable investments against her advice and had placed the future of the estate and their enterprises at considerable risk. Ed had been working hard to turn things around, but the accounts indicated that time was running out and they could no longer wait for the long-anticipated results of his toiling.

Lady Benwick's eldest son, Edwin, had died in a riding accident many years ago. Her youngest son, Ernest and the next Lord Benwick, was a confirmed bachelor who had never expected to inherit. He had taken himself to South America with a group of botanists to study the plant life in those tropical lands, and she had recently received a letter from him officially handing over the running of the estate to his mother and nephew. He found travelling the world and studying plants far more interesting than the boring and burdensome duties of managing the family estate, staff and related business interests. Her expectation of officially becoming the dowager of her family and retiring from handling their family affairs now looked unlikely. She felt stuck in a limbo state.

"Do not patronise me, young man. I am well aware of our financial constraints. Your father, God rest his soul, made some regrettable decisions and your uncle is of no use whatsoever. Which brings me to the inevitable solution..."

Ed eyed her warily as she paused before this new revelation. His grandmother was a wily, old-fashioned relic of her Victorian upbringing and he could read her easily.

He went cold. "No, Grandmama, it's out of the question," he announced firmly.

"I have not spoken," she said, startled by his quick response.

"I am not marrying Esther, Grandmama." *Esther of the plain looks and plain speech* was what he'd called her when they were children. She was the daughter of a family friend whom his grandmother had been hinting at forming an alliance with for years. Looks-wise she was not a patch on his simply delightful and duskily stunning Celia, let alone personality-wise. They had always hated spending any time with her as children, as she had always tried to dominate their play and bully Celia, who had quietly and obstinately refused to do her bidding. "How many times do I have to insist that I desire a love match?"

Lady Benwick sniffed haughtily. "Preposterous idea. You are in no position to indulge in such romantic notions. Edward, my dear, you have great responsibilities. There is the family name to maintain, the estate and the needs of your younger sister to consider. There are school fees to pay and a suitable husband to secure for her."

"We'll manage," he said quietly, almost whispering, as if trying to convince himself as well as his grandmother. Running his hand through his sandy curls, Ed sighed and leaned back in his chair, stretching out his long legs. Celia and Ed had avoided telling his grandmother about their budding relationship and he now bitterly regretted keeping it a secret until Celia could come to terms with the wider implications of a mixed-race relationship.

Exasperated, Lady Benwick huffed, pressed her lips together, and pushed out her chest in irritation. The effect, with her black waistcoat and white blouse, was that she suddenly looked like a penguin, and Ed tried not to laugh out loud. She hated when he teased her. But the smile hovering on his lips disappeared as she continued.

"No, we will not manage. The time for you to take your head out of the sand is long overdue. We need immediate investment, or we will be ruined. This house and the estate have been in the family for generations. Your dratted father left us in this mess." She dabbed her eyes, now brimming with tears, with her handkerchief. "How will I hold my head up in polite society? You know what these people are like," she moaned pitifully.

Ed sprang from his chair, dropped to his knees in front of her, and put his arms around her. He loved and respected his grandmother, but he had long ago thrown away his rose-coloured spectacles. *Ironically, you are all one of a kind, as they are just like you,* Ed thought ruefully, but refrained from making the point out loud.

Recovering slightly and visibly pleased at Ed's show of comfort and affection, Lady Benwick continued in a persuasive voice, "Esther's father is willing to invest a considerable amount into the business or guarantee a loan...and provide a generous dowry." She lifted a delicate Japanese fan from the ebony table beside her chair and waved it dramatically before her flushed, sharp-featured face. "All these benefits will be supplemented by a generous inheritance from her grandfather's estate. It will solve all our problems."

Esther's father ran a prestigious family bank, and her mother was the granddaughter of a West Indian banana merchant. Every suitor who had shown interest in Esther during her season had solely been interested in her vast family fortune and the promise of a generous dowry and marriage portion. Inevitably, her dower personality and domineering mother had put any potential suitors off and she had not been successful in securing a marriage proposal.

"Control of her finances will pass to you, and she will comply with her husband's advice, just as her mother was brought up to do." She reached out and covered his hands with her own. "Promise me you will at least give it some serious thought? Our futures are in your hands, my child."

Ed stared down at the ropes of blue veins in her hands. fear and guilt wrapped around him like a persistent fog. He wanted to drag his hands from the cold vise of her grip. The thought of marrying someone other than Celia sent a shiver down his spine. Marrying Esther would solve all their financial problems, but what about his feelings and plans for the future?

His options were bleak. Either sacrifice his family's future or renege on his commitment to Celia.

Chapter Four

The next day, Celia and Ed stopped at the junction of Tottenham Court Road, Oxford Street, and Charing Cross. What should have been a sunny, bright spring day was marred by the smog from burning coal and the increasing number of manufactories in the city. Despite the time of year, the air was quite chilly and sharp, and Celia had shivered violently whilst carrying out her morning ablutions; even with a warm fire in her bedchamber, getting dressed had been a hurried affair.

Celia wore a smart burgundy ensemble stylishly embellished with sculpted ruffles on the back of a modest bustle and sharp pleating as a feature on the underskirt. Black velvet trim on the cuffs and neck of the jacket complimented the core colour. Carefully lifting her long skirts to navigate the debris-strewn roadway, she allowed Ed to take her elbow. With his other hand on his topper, he guided her across the busy junction full of horse-drawn hansom cabs, wagons and omnibuses being urged forward by drivers anxious to reach their destinations.

A buxom matron dressed in widow's weeds seated in a hansom cab whose driver was taking his time in negotiating the turn from Charing Cross into Oxford Street tutted impatiently, then happened to glance their way; she shook her head disapprovingly.

Celia turned her head and looked up at Ed. "This is why I don't usually link arms with you."

"Ignore the old trout," he said, not bothering to lower his voice.

"Ed, really? You are shocking at times," Celia reprimanded him, struggling to contain her amusement as the middle-aged matron sputtered with outrage.

"It would do her well to mind her own business in future. If people focused half as much on their own affairs rather than the lives of others, the world would be much improved," Ed said crossly, as he concentrated on guiding them across the busy junction.

Once safely across, they strolled along Charing Cross Road. The couple met little fanfare, merely the odd curious look from their fellow citizens. Celia mused on the haphazardness of the reactions they received when out together. It had not mattered much when they were just friends with nothing to hide, but since they had become romantic, although they were careful to act no differently with each other, she now had an increased awareness of the reactions of others.

They stopped outside the bookshop owned by her best friend, Georgia Claremont, and her half-sister, Amelia. Ed pushed the door open and held it for her, the bell dangling above it clanging loudly to announce their entrance. Prior to entering the store, Celia had peered through the thick glass panels on the door and spotted Georgia immediately. She wore a version of what she dubbed her shop uniform: a black and white plaid skirt and a pretty cotton blouse with leg of mutton sleeves and a lacy white collar and matching plaid necktie. Her curly, reddish-brown hair was drawn back into a loose bun, save for a fringe of paper-curled tendrils on her forehead. She was in deep conversation with a smartly dressed gentleman who had his back to them. Something about his demeanour seemed familiar.

Drawn by the sound of the bell, Georgia glanced towards the door and her hazel-flecked grey eyes twinkled as she spotted Celia and Ed. A cheeky smile split her freckled, creamy cheeks. "How lovely to see you both. When did you return to London? Celia, look who's returned to England's shores." She clasped her hands in delight.

"Georgia, will you please take a breath? It's lovely to see you too," Celia said fondly, laughing at her excited friend. Her laughter stopped abruptly, and her eyes enlarged in shock as the gentleman turned around and she recognised him. Did her heart actually skip a beat? Realising her mouth was hanging open, she clamped it shut, embarrassed.

"Celia, it's lovely to see you." He raised his black topper slightly, amused at her response.

Celia nodded stiffly and continued to stare at him in stunned silence. She had not seen this man for a good few years. It had all been so juvenile and childish, just a silly crush, she told herself, but the butterflies fluttering around in her stomach told a different story. Feeling shy, she struggled unsuccessfully to stop gaping at him as if he were the Messiah.

Georgia turned to Ed. "Ed, since Celia seems to have lost her tongue, please allow me to introduce you to an old friend of ours, Nathaniel Thompson. Nathan, this is Edward Langdon."

Celia managed to drag her eyes away from Nathan's mesmerising dark gaze as the two men shook hands in greeting. Thankfully, the bookshop had relatively few customers, none of whom she knew. They all seemed to be primarily focused on the books on display, rather than her awkward behaviour. Georgia's salesclerk, Tom, was handling their needs.

Recovering slightly, she offered up a quick prayer of thanks and managed to pull herself together. If her dark brown skin had been two shades lighter, she was convinced that the fiery heat rising up her cheekbones would have been accompanied by a flaming red blush.

"Ed." She slipped one slender brown hand lightly into the crook of his elbow, ignoring his quick glance of surprise at this unusual public display of affection. "Georgia and I met Nathan at a fundraising temperance lecture for freedmen a few years back and became fast friends. He moved to New York not long after we all met."

Smiling defiantly, she observed Nathan's narrow-eyed reaction to her intimate gesture. Feeling slightly shamed for acting so childishly out of character, she blamed it on Nathan for his sudden reappearance in her life. How dare he return to England after he had betrayed her trust, and greet her as if they had just spoken yesterday?

"Mmm...interesting you've never mentioned him, Celia," Ed said, glancing from one to the other in bewilderment. The tension simmering between Nathan and Celia was so thick, she knew he could sense it.

Nathan cleared his throat and smiled tightly. "Well, I can assure you I have heard many delightful stories about your childhood friendship. May I introduce you to my daughter, Elouise?" He gently tried to pull forward a child that Celia noticed for the first time, hiding behind him. A cheeky, copper-toned face with large, dark brown eyes, long black pigtails, and an impish smile peeked at them from behind his open frock coat, but the girl shyly refused to be manoeuvred into an introduction.

Consumed with shock, Celia could see the adorable little minx was the spitting image of her striking father, who, she noted, being a few years older and more mature, was even more handsome. She surreptitiously took in his tall, lithe figure, wide shoulders, strong, square jaw and glowing skin. His expertly tailored turquoise waistcoat emphasised his broad chest, narrow waist, and slim hips to perfection.

"Louise, really. Come now. This is not the time to play peek-a-boo, my darling," Nathan scolded gently. His daughter giggled and jumped back behind him, then peeped out at Celia again.

Laughing, Nathan heaved her up into his arms as if she were feather light. The little girl wrapped her arms around his neck and hid her face. She wore an adorable white sailor outfit with blue trimmings and stripes. "My apologies. She is a little shy amongst strangers. Although we're bombarded with nonstop chatter when we are at home or in familiar company. Isn't that right, young lady?" He looked down at her fondly and she nodded bashfully.

"Hello, Elouise—or is it Louise?" Celia asked, observing the interaction between father and daughter and noting the 'we're' in his sentence. There was no sign of her mother in the bookshop and Celia had no intention of letting him know she had any interest in her whereabouts.

"It's Elouise, ma'am." Louise had pulled her head from her father's neck and turned towards Celia to answer the question politely. Smiling self-consciously, she buried her head back into her father's neck. They all laughed heartily, breaking the awkward tension that had momentarily taken over the friendly atmosphere of the bookshop.

"Well, despite the fact that I'm unable to view your adorable little face for more than a second or two, it's lovely to finally meet you," Celia replied. She loved children and got on very well with Ed's younger sister, Charlotte. She had no intention of holding the sins of the father against the child, she thought sanctimoniously. Celia sighed inwardly and scolded herself for feeling so petty towards Nathan. This was so unlike her. What was happening to her?

Nathan smiled at her gratefully, clearly relieved at her response, admiration shining in his eyes. Celia avoided his gaze and continued to smile beneficently at Louise, who was indeed an adorable little girl.

"I think this little minx is getting tired. We should be getting along now. It's been lovely to reacquaint myself with you and Georgia. Edward, good to meet you." Nathan inclined his head.

Ed returned the nod. "Good to meet you, too. Just call me Ed, no need for formalities."

Nathan smiled courteously and departed the store with Louise waving to everyone like the Great Queen of Sheba waving to her subjects, suddenly confident now that she knew they were leaving. They all laughed at the regal display.

"Is there something you wish to tell me?" Georgia looked sharply at the slender hand still resting in the crook of Ed's elbow.

"Not at the moment, no. Have you been decorating?" Celia responded quickly. Avoiding both their eyes, she gazed around the store and found herself staring at the ceiling with great interest. It had recently been painted professionally rather than wallpapered and looked fresh and clean compared to its previous dull finish.

"Well, whatever's going on, I do hope you both know what you're getting into." Georgia gave up her weak attempt at interrogation, knowing Celia could be quite obstinate if she did not want to discuss something.

Ed remained silent as the two young women caught up on other matters of the female variety, taking advantage of their distraction to admire Celia. She was slim and above average height for a woman, yet she managed to balance this out with her voluptuous figure. She had a pair of very large, very pretty dark brown eyes that lent her an appearance of innocence, but Ed knew there was a sharp mind behind them. His gaze paused, fascinated as always, on the tiny smattering of freckles across her turned-up nose, an endearing contrast to her otherwise clear, deeply chocolate skin.

Sighing, he turned away, deciding to purchase a popular literary novel for his grandmother. But as he made his way over to Tom the salesclerk, who was standing by two glass cases displaying a range of stationery, journals and cards he frowned. What was behind the awkward atmosphere between Celia and Nathan, and how would it impact their relationship, now he had returned. Considering his own dilemma, which had been forced upon him by his grandmother, could he dare to ask her such a question without revealing his own inner conflict?

Chapter Five

Celia lay on her back in her half-canopied bed, staring at the ceiling of her dimly lit bedchamber. The faint light from the moon and the fading coals in the fireplace created soft shadows around the room.

She knew she was blessed to have a boudoir, small sitting area and tiny dressing room on the second floor of the townhouse. Since reaching adulthood, Celia had spent more time in London than at the country estate. Lady Benwick had allowed her to personalise the accessories and soft furnishings in the room to her taste, which Celia had insisted on paying for out of her inheritance. She had succeeded in creating a warm and welcoming ambience with an exotic mix of terra cotta, blues, greens and golds, which softened the predominantly ebonised furniture.

Celia pulled at the eiderdown with one hand and drew it up carefully, so she would not disturb the half-naked man dozing, half beside her, half draped over her. His face rested on the low frilled decolletage of her sleeveless cotton nightgown. One long, olive-toned arm was flung across it, and a pyjama clad leg rested lightly across both of hers.

If Lady Benwick and polite society could see them, they would be utterly scandalised. She and Ed would be banished from the kingdom, and she would be branded a shameless hussy, even though she was a mature adult and financially independent. She pressed her lips together to stop herself from bursting out in laughter at the thought of their hypocritical faces. Some of the stories she had heard over the years about the carryings on of the gentry would make this scenario look as innocent as a walk in the park.

Celia shivered with pleasure as Ed lightly stroked the soft skin of her thigh through the thin fabric of the nightgown, then softly kissed and snuggled into her neck. This was the second opportunity they had had to spend a whole night together. The first time had been months ago, at Lady Benwick's country house.

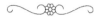

Lady Benwick had gone to stay the night with the dreadful Esther and her family in Essex. Earlier in the evening, Celia had written a passage in her journal and after completing her nightly ablutions, she had sat at her vanity table, plaiting her long black hair into four neat canerows. She smiled ironically as the nightly process triggered a distant memory of her parents jovially debating whether the broad range of ancestral braiding styles should be called cornrows, the more popular American term, or canerows, the term traditionally used in the Caribbean islands by coloured people.

Just as she got to the end of one thick plait of tightly curled hair, the door had clicked gently, and Ed had slipped into the room. She had expected him.

It was late; the staff were all in bed and he had told his valet, James Harris, not to bother to wait up for him when he had left for an evening at one of his gentleman's clubs; ironically, the type of establishment that her father and some of his non-aristocratic white ancestors would most likely have never been allowed to enter, and probably would not wish to.

Ed had seen the headscarf she would normally have covered her braids with on many occasions through the years, but she had not worn her headscarf that night, as it would have killed any romantic notions. Their eyes had met in the vanity table's gilded mirror as he silently strolled up behind her. There had been no need for words. They smiled secretly at each other, and she had stood up to greet him with a deep kiss. He had scooped her up and carried her over to the bed, then pressed his well-toned body against hers, covering her face and neck with soft kisses.

Every touch and tantalising kiss created a tide of emotions that carried them dangerously closer to full intimacy. Celia had exercised some much-needed restraint by tickling Ed in all of the most treacherous places, sending the both of them into muffled fits of laughter. She was all too aware of what could happen if they had allowed their emotions to get out of hand, and who would carry the major burden of any indiscretions.

Although Celia could no longer consider herself completely innocent, they had never been fully intimate. They were both determined that she would only give up her full innocence on her marriage bed and not a minute before. There was too much at stake.

Celia had come to the conclusion that she should put her doubts aside and accept Ed's marriage proposal, but he had suddenly been quite distant and seemed troubled, which had once again made her hesitant. Neither of them had had time to bring up the subject of marriage since his proposal a few weeks before, as they had both been distracted by their various responsibilities. *Has he changed his mind, or are the problems with the haulage business still weighing heavily on his mind?* It was all rather odd and in complete contrast to their intimacy tonight. The intensity and emotion had been explosive. *So where are we going wrong? Are we confusing lust with love?* No wonder she was so indecisive.

Celia had needed the physical intimacy and comfort, as they had not really had any real time alone for months. It had not helped that since seeing Nathan, she had also been feeling vulnerable and confused, as all her old insecurities linked to his rejection came rushing back to her. Should true love be this difficult? Regarding the issues of race, she could take a deep breath and face the world, but what about the other doubts that kept creeping up out of nowhere, like ivy shrouding the walls of an old country house?

Celia yawned and closed her eyes. She would not sleep tonight. They would need to be awake well before she was due to ring the bell for the chambermaid to come for her daily ritual in the morning.

"But surely there must be someone suitable that you have in mind, Celia? You are such a sociable creature, m'dear. Are you trying to convince me that between all those jubilee singing concerts for American freedmen, charitable committees and assisting in the bookshop you have not met one suitable young man?" Lady Benwick pressed as she placed her cutlery together on her clean plate to signify that she had finished her breakfast. She had a healthy appetite and did not approve of people leaving food on plates, particularly when so many impoverished of the land were starving in the streets or in workhouses. Removing her napkin from her lap she pressed it to her lips.

Exasperated, Celia silently raised her eyes to heaven and hid her simmering vexation by concentrating on completing the last remnants of her delicious breakfast. It had been prepared by the agency cook, Mrs Watson, whom she had employed for Lady Benwick for the duration of their London stay.

"Thank you," she said to Jenny, as the housemaid poured fresh coffee into their cups, and to James the valet, as he cleared their plates and silverware. Apart from Jenny pressing her lips together once when catching Celia's rolling eyes, neither of them betrayed any trace of their inward amusement as they carried out their duties. They were used to Lady Benwick quizzing her now adult wards over the dining table for various reasons and of course it would be unprofessional to display any personal reaction.

This was a familiar conversation that her bewildered guardian brought up every so often since Celia had come of age. Celia was used to it and patiently indulged it, believing that deep down the elderly lady was just lonely and, having endured an unhappy arranged marriage, she was somewhat jaded by her own life experiences. Celia would always be grateful to her for agreeing to be her guardian. Although she had never been particularly warm or affectionate, she had always ensured that Celia had wanted for nothing materially.

Celia had graciously explained earlier in the conversation that she had not been attracted to any of the decent suitors that had been introduced to her and did not intend to defend her stance further. She had been in a sunny mood for the past two days and was still glowing from the night she had spent with Ed. Nothing was going to spoil her euphoria, especially not a pointless debate about her apparent lack of romantic pursuits.

Familiar with Celia's obstinance when she did not wish to discuss something, more so if she considered the subject too personal, a frustrated Lady Benwick turned her gimlet eye to Ed. He was helping himself to a second serving of food from a narrow sideboard jammed with an array of silver serving dishes.

"Edward, as usual, you are clamped to the sideboard. Do you have to persist in eating lashings of food at every meal? It borders on the unseemly." She sniffed.

"Waste not, want not, Grandmama. You taught me well." Ed grinned, his handsome face lighting up as he helped himself to a generous selection of eggs, bacon, and cold meats left over from the last evening's meal.

Celia bit her bottom lip to stop a sly smile from appearing. No doubt the card game last night with his cronies, accompanied by generous glasses of brandy, had worked up an appetite. *Just as their delicious rendezvous in her boudoir two nights before had worked up his appetite at breakfast the following morning,* she thought, secretly revelling in the delicious memory.

Ed gave her an indiscreet wink as he sat back down at the breakfast table to attack his meal with impeccable manners. Celia's answering smile disappeared as she realised that Lady Benwick had turned her rheumy, bespectacled eyes back to her.

For a usually sensible, no-nonsense matron, the short-sighted Lady Benwick was too vain to wear her spectacles in public, as they made her eyes look beady. She insisted on squinting behind a pair of modish lorgnette opera glasses—when she remembered to carry them.

"Well?" Lady Benwick studied Celia intently. "Please don't take this the wrong way, but you must surely wish to have a family one day soon?" She turned her head to one side to regard Celia.

"Of course, Lady B," Celia sighed, using the private nickname she had picked up from Ed. Lady Benwick had been amused by the pet name bestowed on her by her favourite grandchild, and did not mind Celia and Charlotte using it, even though Ed no longer did. However, Celia had tired of her persistent questioning. Not wishing to be rude, she sipped at her black coffee, inhaling the full aroma as she appreciated the sweetness from the several lumps of sugar she had added to counteract the bitterness.

Celia's single status had been a bone of contention for many years as she had many white suitors from respectable families. It was all to Lady Benwick's surprise in view of Celia's race and ward status. But Celia had not wished to put her inheritance in jeopardy. Despite the Divorce and Marriage Acts coming into existence during the mid and latter half of the 19th century, women had few rights in practice, as men could still control their finances in certain circumstances. Many women preferred to defer to their husbands, fathers or other male relatives for financial advice and management; whether they were qualified to provide such guidance was another matter. After seeking legal advice, she had placed a good proportion of her inheritance in a wider range of investments. This and any potential business venture would be entirely in her own name.

Since coming into her inheritance, she had not really had time to investigate suitable ventures, as she had fallen into the comfortable routine of acting as Lady Benwick's companion and supplementary housekeeper. She had also wished to enjoy some of her freedoms as a financially independent woman. Another dilemma had been her living accommodations. Ideally, she needed a business with living quarters above and at least one female staff member to assist her with cooking and household duties, and possibly some of her business activities.

Deep down, Celia had to admit that the thought of breaking away from the family had both excited and terrified her. Apart from her beloved parents and her best friend, Georgia, they were all she had known since she had been a young and vulnerable girl who was in need of their support and protection. Her paternal uncle, who lived in Bristol with his Irish wife and children, ran a public house with his father-in-law. Celia visited them at least once a year when she could, but there had never been any thought of her living with them. He had such a large brood that she would just have been an extra mouth to feed.

Her maternal aunt in New York lived in Harlem. She taught at one of the many schools financed through temperance lectures and concerts set up, post slavery, in the style of the legendary black American Fisk Jubilee singers. Celia corresponded with her regularly, but distance had prevented them from becoming close.

She had grown up with Ed and his family, spending more time with them than with her own in the years her father and godfather had been alive. Lady Benwick had always been somewhat distant, as was her nature, but she had been close to her godparents, Ed and Charlotte, who was now away at school. She enjoyed reading Charlotte's letters, filled with stories of her friendships, midnight feasts and classroom pranks, which made her and Ed scream with laughter, recalling their own experiences at boarding school.

Her old school friend Georgia and her sister Amelia were like family to her too. They had gone through many trials and tribulations due to their mixed heritage and what was seen as dubious parentage; that dubious parentage referred to a coloured mother and white father who had been a colonial high-ranking diplomat. They had also shared many joyous occasions during their time at Lady Ward's School for Young Ladies in West London.

"Well, you would succeed in securing a husband by actually showing interest in qualifying suitors," Lady Benwick huffed impatiently. She held up her hand as Celia opened her mouth to reply. "I'm well aware that being coloured may cause certain difficulties in some quarters. However, I must say you are a strikingly pretty girl by any healthy alpha male's standards, so I do not want to hear any excuses." She smiled serenely at Celia, who had clamped her mouth shut, her eyes round with surprise.

Celia was secretly touched by the compliment, even if it was somewhat backhanded. But this was Lady Benwick, so what more could she expect? Any endorsement coming from her was practically akin to being told you may be in line for a knighthood. If women were able to receive one, she would have been up there with the best of Queen Victoria's subjects.

"Thank you, ma'am," Celia said, looking at Ed out of the corner of her eye, amused at his increasingly concerned expression.

"Grandmama, would you stop embarrassing Celia? Marriage is not the be all and end all of life, I'll have you know," he snapped as his grandmother studiously ignored him and kept her gaze on her ward.

Celia managed to abstain from spluttering into her coffee as she stared at Ed in surprise. Where had that rhetoric sprung from? She narrowed her eyes. *Are my niggling doubts about our relationship justified? Where did this sudden fair-weather attitude towards marriage spring from?*

As the questions continued to churn around in her mind, she distanced herself from the conversation at the table.

"Celia—Celia?" Lady Benwick shifted impatiently in her seat.

Celia was reluctantly drawn out of her musings.

"Will you cease your daydreaming and pay attention?" Lady Benwick remonstrated, clapping her hands like a performing seal to gain Celia's attention. "A Mr Nathaniel

Thompson has returned to London from New York. I believe he may be a perfect suitor for you."

"Did you say Nathaniel?" Celia enquired in disbelief. Lady Benwick had achieved her goal in securing Celia's undivided attention with the last name she had ever expected to hear around the family breakfast table.

"Indeed. So, you were listening. And what a positively agreeable and handsome young gentlemen he is. He certainly lives up to my exacting standards, based on some discreet inquiries." She placed her hands in her lap and studied Celia with a deceptively innocent look. "He is a blackamoor, he is educated, he is from a wealthy, connected family in Sierra Leone, he is..."

Celia rolled her eyes, squirming at the list of attributes Lady Benwick reeled off in her usual patronising tone. In particular, she tried unsuccessfully to suppress an inward bubble of laughter at the old-fashioned blackamoor term. It was so typical of her guardian to slip back into terms she was more familiar with, despite their falling into disuse in society at large. Lady Benwick stubbornly acted as if it was only yesterday that they had entered the 19th century. *Maybe she took a drop of tipple like Rip Van Winkle,* Celia thought mischievously, *and suddenly awakened in the present day, leapfrogging past the beginning of the century.* She longed to say something, but rather than mocking her guardian, she held her tongue out of respect for the elderly lady.

Lady Benwick ignored her stifled laughter and continued to list Nathan's favourable attributes. Celia held back a sigh. She seemed to sigh continuously when in the presence of her guardian and Ed these days. Thinking about Nathan and his rejection merely induced her to sigh even more. To imagine she had fancied herself in love with him at one time! She felt her cheeks heat at the shame.

They had shared an innocent kiss, after which he had implied that he wished to officially court her—once he returned from a three month visit to New York to see his uncle and oversee some of his business interests there.

The long and short of it was that he managed to get the daughter of a prominent coloured doctor and colleague of Nathan's uncle, with child in the short time he had been in New York. The family name and reputation could not be tarnished with such a scandal; a quick marriage had been arranged.

Being an honest sort, Nathan had written to Celia to apologise for his indiscretion and inform her of his newly married status. He had subtly implied the reason, simply by stating that they would be expecting a child. Although she had been devasted by the news, they had continued to correspond in an ad hoc manner for a little while after, innocently discussing the state of coloured people around the world for the most part, and mundane day to day subjects. They had never referred to what had happened between them in the past. After a short while she had asked him to stop writing to her and to concentrate on supporting his family, for all their sakes.

Celia had not heard anything from Nathan again until they had been reacquainted in Georgia's bookshop. By this time, she had put the experience down to innocent puppy love on her part, completely forgetting about the strong chemistry between them, akin to an electric current. Once she and Ed had fallen for each other and she stopped seeing Ed as some sort of godbrother figure, she had been fooled into a false sense of emotional security by distance and time. How could what could only be lust compare to a lifetime of friendship and, more recently, romantic love that had been nurtured with Ed? Yet could she honestly compare the feelings that both men inspired in her? They were so dissimilar from each other. And if she was being completely honest, she had no idea if the love she shared with Ed was authentic or merely lust. So where did that leave her?

As Lady Benwick ran out of attributes to assign to Nathan, Celia addressed her, determined to set the record straight.

"I know him, Lady B. He is not suitable as he is married, with a child." Celia cleared her throat, avoiding her guardian's eyes. Lady Benwick would not be amused if she learnt of her clandestine meetings with Nathan, even if they were so long ago that they no longer mattered.

"My dear, you cannot know him too well, if you were not aware that he is now a widower," Lady Benwick said, openly triumphant at Celia's bewildered expression.

"Grandmama, that's enough. Why do you insist on embarrassing poor Celia with these tiresome conversations every few months?" Ed scolded her through gritted teeth. He had finished his hearty breakfast and had been preparing to excuse himself, but his patience had run out. "Allow both of us to manage our own affairs of the heart and kindly change the subject."

Lady Benwick eyed them both, lips compressed in disapproval. Celia smiled gratefully at Ed, though she wondered why he had inserted himself into the request, considering she was the only one being harangued.

"Very well. I shall cease my well-intentioned advice for the time being, Celia." Lady Benwick smiled coldly at Celia's undisguised look of relief and turned to Edward. "My dear, would you please make yourself useful and see about someone refilling the coffee pot," she said primly. "Jenny and James seem to have disappeared down the rabbit hole and I wish to discuss some household issues with Celia."

She turned to Celia. "Now Mrs Watson has found her feet, I wonder if you would mind organising an intimate dinner party."

Ed scowled and hurriedly excused himself.

"Is everything alright, Ed?" Celia asked, drawing her eyebrows together in concern.

"Of course, he's alright," Lady Benwick said, smiling smugly.

Celia frowned doubtfully as she watched him stride toward the door. *Well...really. Hmm. If he insists on overeating at breakfast, then once again his stomach will protest in response.*

Ed used the tapestry bell pull by the door to summon the staff before swiftly retreating from the room.

"Well?" Lady Benwick said impatiently, awaiting Celia's answer.

Celia turned her attention back to Lady Benwick, relieved that the subject had been changed to a dinner party, an event that she would enjoy and was more than capable of arranging. "Of course. For how many?"

"Just Mr and Mrs Coleville, their daughter Esther, Edward and I," Lady Benwick replied, patting her neatly coiffed silver strands.

Celia's heart sank. "I'm not expected to attend?" she enquired hopefully.

"No, my dear. Let us not pretend that you are Mrs Coleville's favourite person. And I am well aware that the feeling is mutual." Lady Benwick had confirmed Celia's suspicions. She was disliked intensely by Mrs. Coleville—and Esther, for that matter—and had merely been tolerated as the family's ward.

As the only grandchild of a West Indian planter, Mrs Coleville had inherited the bulk of his fortune and his bigotry. Her superior attitude towards people of colour and those of the lower orders was legendary. Rumour had it that, while she had married for love, her husband had only married her for her fortune, and her poor servants took the brunt of her bitterness, especially the ones who hailed from the colonies.

Coloured servants had long been a staple and symbol of wealth and status, particularly during the previous two centuries. The fashion was dying out due to the abolition of slavery that saw people of colour leaving the port cities of Britain. Nevertheless, old habits die hard and recruitment of servants of colour remained popular amongst professional colonial families and those in the nobility and gentry who had historical and cultural links to various parts of the colonies.

"Well, I will not speak ill of either of them, but I certainly do not wish to spend time with people who merely tolerate me," Celia replied. "Would you like some West Indian dishes included in the menu?"

"Yes, I was hoping you would make some suggestions that would be appropriate for this occasion. I think the main course should be British with a few French delicacies," Lady Benwick clarified. "However, we need to ensure the menu is balanced out with a few spicy Jamaican dishes—possibly starters and a selection of desserts."

"Maybe a lobster or pumpkin soup for starters?" Celia suggested.

Lady Benwick nodded. Celia continued to make suggestions for the desserts and the main course, happy in the knowledge that she would not have to attend the dinner and spend time with the frightful Mrs Coleville and her daughter.

Celia wondered if Edward had been informed about this intimate dinner. Was that why he had left the room in such a hurry? Inwardly, she smirked, then grimaced as she imagined his horror at having to break bread with Esther and her mother. *Poor Ed*. In contrast, as an old family friend, Mr Coleville had always been a jovial, friendly type, so different from his wife and daughter. *God help the pitiful soul who marries into that family.*

Chapter Six

"Amelia is preparing herself to become a mail order bride for some cowboy in the Wild West of America."

"Sorry, did I just hear you correctly?" Celia placed *The Count of Monte Cristo* by Alexandre Dumas on the empty seat beside her. They had been discussing the famous author's fascinating African ancestry and the extraordinary story of his mulatto father, Thomas-Alexandre, the son of a French nobleman and a Caribbean slave, Marie Dumas. Thomas-Alexandre had been the first general of African ancestry in the French army and had served with distinction.

Sitting regally on the wing chair opposite, Georgia grimaced, wrinkling her little snub nose, then grinned at Celia's puzzled expression and the widening of her large, almond-shaped eyes. "Yes, you heard me perfectly well. She is right at this moment on a visit to our beloved brother and father to reveal her plans to him. My father and his current wife are already privy to her madness and are understandably horrified."

Celia smiled mischievously as she was well aware that Georgia and Amelia's prissy older brother was a snob of the highest order and there was no love lost between him and his younger sisters. As for their father and stepmother, they were barely in their lives due to distance and parental apathy. Suffice to say, they were not a close family.

"I see...," Celia said, for once quite speechless.

They were sitting in Georgia's neat little parlour above the bookshop. It was a cosy space with delicate furnishings upholstered in plush pink, purple and terra cotta velvet. The two sofas and lone chair clashed fashionably with the green vines of the wallpaper and gold satin cushions. The seventeenth century mahogany writing bureau standing in the corner by one of the bright, high windows lent the room the only hint of masculinity. It had been left to her by her beloved paternal grandfather.

Celia had escaped the townhouse for the evening. The dreadful Esther and her mother were attending the intimate dinner party that she had arranged for Lady Benwick. Thankfully, it had coincided with a meeting of the literary society that she and Georgia had founded and run for the past few years. Only Georgia and Celia were in attendance this time, as Amelia was spending time with her father and incorrigible stepmother. Their father was still recovering from a bout of pneumonia, and she wished to ensure that he was being looked after. Tom, Georgia's salesclerk, had other plans that evening.

Nathan had also attended before he had moved to New York, and when he was not busy with his parish duties, Mr Henderson, the rather handsome curate, also attended. For some reason there always seemed to be some bone of contention between Georgia and Mr Henderson. Celia could not quite put her finger on it, but she was sure she would get to the bottom of the matter one day.

"Aren't you going to ask me how, what, where, when, etcetera? You're usually peppering me with questions I cannot possibly answer. On the one occasion I have a wealth of information for you, you let me down." Georgia glared at Celia in mock outrage whilst smoothing imaginary creases from her lace-panelled grey skirt.

Celia giggled and held her palms up in a defensive pose. "Forgive me if I'm still reeling from the shock. I'm also quite tired from the concert last night." She politely covered her mouth and stifled a yawn. Georgia smiled at Celia sympathetically.

The night before, they had thoroughly enjoyed a concert given by the East London Jubilee Singers and another black choral group from one of the Southern states in America. Both groups were styled after the famous Fisk Jubilee Singers, who back in the 1870s had raised money to build and create Fisk University by travelling across America and Europe. They had even performed for Queen Victoria and other notable members of the aristocracy and government.

Following the abolition of the slave trade in America in the late 1860s, individuals and organisations, such as the Freedman's Bureau, had established schools, colleges, churches and other essential institutions for recently freed slaves and existing free men, women and children.

During the 1870s, a large part of the Western world, including Britain and other countries in Europe, were introduced to the folk songs and Negro spirituals of Black America. They were all the rage at the time and remained quite popular. The temperance movement was also an integral part of these concerts and campaigns of awareness, as abstaining from alcohol was seen as a significant aspect of advancing coloured communities. Self-improvement and abstinence were intrinsically linked to abolition and progress, post-abolition.

"It was such fun, wasn't it?" Georgia clapped her childlike hands joyfully. "We must attend the next one. The temperance lecturer was rather passionate. It was interesting to see so many people from all walks of life. It just shows that like-minded people can come together on common issues, regardless of race, class or gender."

Celia nodded vigorously. "It was uplifting and informative. Those concerts are always enjoyable, and it's lovely to be able to donate to a great cause. So many people across America who have been struggling to adapt to their new freedoms and access resources will benefit greatly."

"Yes, it's a disgrace the way the race has been treated over there in the years since Reconstruction. This segregation business is terrifying. It's a shameful setback. I thought it could be challenging here, navigating prejudice socially, in industry and legislatively. It's especially quite violent for the men at times. However, nothing here compares to the extent of oppression of our people in the Americas."

Celia nodded sadly. "Come to think of it, most of the extremely evil strategies and oppressive regimes practised by this country's government seem to have the most impact in the colonies, rather than here. Justice, kindness and tolerance are merely smoke and mirrors."

They sat in silent thought for a moment.

"By the way," Celia said, "I recently received a letter from my aunt who lives in New York. The colour bar is difficult enough there. Can you imagine how it is in the South and other parts of the country? No wonder so many coloured people are fleeing to the West and Midwest to create settlements and homesteads."

"It's very worrying. I don't want to think about how it will be for Amelia. I keep hoping she changes her mind." Worry creased the creamy skin on Georgia's forehead.

Post Reconstruction, it seemed that the steady progress of black people was being set back by systematic and local marginalisation and disenfranchisement. Many members of the Republican party, the popular party of choice for the race, and the opposing Democrats were actively stopping people from voting. Votes were also being suppressed or not counted.

Schools were off limits to black students. Localised violence against black communities by racist mobs was commonplace. Large numbers of blacks in the South were fleeing to the American West and Midwest, to places like Wyoming, Kansas and Colorado where they set up diverse or mainly black communities. Many areas in these territories were also racist, but not to the extent of the South. There were negative systematic, educational and social impacts to a certain extent, but nothing like the sadistic oppression and violence, including lynching, being enacted increasingly in the South without any civil or legal repercussions.

Celia sighed in exasperation. "Oh, let's change the subject. It's not all doom and gloom by far. So many positives have come out of fighting for our freedoms, and we must continue to support their endeavours in building self-sufficient communities and educating both young and old. I love to hear about the success stories of the race in the face of adversity. Don't you?"

"Indeed. It was nice to see so many familiar faces, was it not?" Georgia gladly switched the subject back to the previous night's American fundraising soiree. She peeped at Celia slyly from under her long auburn lashes. Her hazel green eyes sparkled with mischief.

Celia smiled innocently. "Oh yes, Mr Henderson looked dashing, don't you think?" Celia fluttered her eyelashes and fanned herself dramatically with her Japanese hand-painted fan.

Georgia grimaced and rolled her eyes. "Mr Henderson? I was referring to our handsome Nathan, not that insufferable know-it-all."

"Doth thou protest too much, my dear?" Celia replied knowingly, ignoring the heat rising up her high cheekbones at the mention of Nathan's name.

"Just admit that Nathan was dashing and handsome, my dear, and let us change the subject immediately," Georgia announced bluntly, cutting her eyes at Celia in irritation.

Momentarily locking gazes with eyes for daggers, they abruptly burst into fits of laughter, no longer able to contain their amusement at the other's observations. The sunny vibrations of their mirth highlighted the warmth of their sisterly comradery.

"Celia, behave! You cannot call a curate dashing," Georgia protested, trying to catch her breath.

"Why not, if that's what he is? He was a thoroughly disreputable, handsome and dashing rake of the highest order in his youth. It's hardly a secret."

Georgia nodded grudgingly. "I have to admit that his character has changed, at least on the surface. Who knows what passions lurk underneath that cool exterior and reserve?"

"I'm convinced I can feel something simmering whenever you're in his presence," Celia replied with faux coyness.

"Nonsense." Georgia waved her hand dismissively, a faint flush rising above her white lace collar.

Celia decided to take pity on her friend, selfishly hoping the subject of Nathan would also be squashed in the process. "So what, pray tell, led Amelia to want to make this mad escapade across America?"

Georgia cleared her throat, relieved at the unexpected shift in subject to the unspoken romantic intentions of her elder sister. "She is desperate to settle down and start a family. As you know, the choices in London are limited due to our dubious parentage."

Celia sympathised. The options for marriage were scarce for a young woman born out of wedlock to her father's African servant. Even though her now retired father had been an esteemed diplomat and member of the gentry, he had been notorious for seducing his female servants of any race, hence the existence of Georgia. Goodness knew how many other illegitimate children he had scattered around, as he had acknowledged Georgia for reasons known only to himself, and he rarely discussed her mother.

Amelia had been born to her housekeeper mother who had been in a previous marriage to the son of an esteemed local chief. She had left her father-in-law's thriving chiefdom when, after his son's death, it had been implied that she should create a union with a distant cousin she had no feelings for. The widow met Georgia's father, then a widower, when he had taken a position with the colonial government in Sierra Leone. He had insisted that Amelia, who had been living with her maternal grandparents whilst her mother worked as a housekeeper, should now grow up in the same household as Georgia; he would become Amelia's benefactor.

Devastated when Georgia's mother died shortly after her birth due to complications, he had moved back to England. He had ensured the two girls received the best education and lacked for nothing financially, despite the disapproval of society and their elder brother, who had been conceived in their father's first marriage and was outraged at this turn of events. As far as their brother was concerned, what had happened in Africa should have stayed in Africa.

Georgia and Amelia had become firm friends with Celia while attending Lady Ward's School for Young Ladies. When they finished school, he had set them up with the stationery shop, the apartments above, a housekeeper and a housemaid.

Although they hardly knew him, they loved their father, as he had been warm and affectionate when they were young. When he had remarried, he had become distant, apparently ruled with an iron fist by his pious and wealthy new wife.

"When is Amelia leaving for this adventure in the wilderness? Did you say she was moving to the Wild West?"

Georgia frowned. "Too soon. Her passage is booked for next month. I will miss her terribly."

"I'm so sorry, Georgia. I know it isn't much compensation, but you know I'm always here for you."

Georgia smiled fondly at Celia. "Thank you, my dear. You know you've always been like another sister to me. I have the best memories of our escapades at school."

"Mostly instigated by you," Celia reminded her.

Georgia smirked. "Of course. Heaven knows how I managed to avoid being expelled."

That prompted more joyous laughter.

Georgia wiped the tears from her eyes with her neatly embroidered grey handkerchief. "Actually, this whole sorry debacle brings me to a little proposition..."

Celia examined her friend curiously, her large brown eyes narrowing. "What are you up to now, Georgia? Come now, spit it out."

Georgia grinned. "Me? When am I ever up to anything?"

"I take it you've forgotten your earlier confession about schoolgirl escapades already?" Celia said, rolling her eyes in amusement and kissing her teeth at her friend's feigned ignorance.

"Would you consider purchasing Amelia's share in the business and moving into the apartments with me?" Georgia asked.

Celia could not suppress her joy at being asked. "I'm flattered that you would consider me, and it would satisfy my desire to invest my inheritance in a venture of some sort. But do you mind if I have a think about it and seek some legal advice first?"

"Of course. There really is no rush. It's a life-changing step both financially and personally," Georgia replied.

Celia breathed a sigh of relief at Georgia's practical nature. She thought about Ed and wondered if this chance at independence may be the answer to their relationship problems. They could conduct their romance for a little longer without the risk of Lady Benwick finding out. If they were going to move forward with their relationship, she would need to discuss Georgia's business proposal with him first. After all, there was no urgency to get married. Or was she using the situation to procrastinate again and ignore her doubts about the relationship?

Chapter Seven

Celia knew it was wrong to eavesdrop, but after returning from the literary society meeting and checking on Mrs Watson in the kitchen, she had walked upstairs and heard Mrs Coleville's loud monotone voice on the other side of the saloon door. The woman sounded unusually joyful, which made Celia curious.

"So when can we announce the happy occasion?" Esther's mother asked.

Celia frowned. What was the annoying harridan referring to?

"Steady on," Ed said, and Celia heard the alarm in his baritone voice. Peeping through the gap in the door, Celia could see his look of dismay and the determined look on Mrs Coleville's ruddy face.

What on earth?

"I haven't come to a decision yet," Ed clarified.

Celia forced herself not to burst into the room. *What decision?*

Mrs Coleville bristled.

"But what is there to decide, Ed? You know how much our families have longed for a union by marriage," said Esther irritably. "This is hardly news to you. Or is there someone else in the picture?"

Celia listened with dread in her heart. She felt as if it had dropped in her chest, it felt so heavy.

"Of course not," Lady Benwick quickly interjected. Ed paled slightly and pulled on his stiff white collar. His grandmother's face looked pinched.

Esther huffed impatiently.

"My dear, allow Ed the courtesy of taking his time to make such a life-changing decision. Marriage should not be taken lightly," Esther's father said.

"Whose side are you on, Father?" Esther shot back with barely controlled rage at his interference.

"This is not about sides, Esther. Marriage is a lifetime commitment that both parties need to be happy with. I don't wish you to have any regrets."

Mrs Coleville shot her husband a piercing look. "What is that supposed to mean? Are you referring to our union?"

Still listening behind the door, Celia smirked with satisfaction, remembering the older couple had had an arranged marriage of sorts. *Of course, he's referring to you, you interfering old bat.*

"Now, now, my dear. Of course not! Please refrain from upsetting yourself," Esther's father replied hurriedly. "I'm just ensuring that these young people know exactly what they are getting into."

"Really, Mother, this is not the time and place to reflect on your own marriage. Our marriage will be full of love and happiness. Won't it, Ed?" Esther gave Ed a simpering smile.

Ed cleared his throat and caught his grandmother's eye. He looked like he was crying out for help.

"Let Ed get used to the idea for a little longer. I'm sure he will eventually come around to our way of thinking," Lady Benwick said reassuringly.

Celia had had enough. She knocked on the door and entered the saloon regally, a look of pure innocence on her face, until she discreetly shot a poisonous look at Ed. Ignoring the dismay in his eyes as he realised that she had overheard them, Celia nodded and smiled serenely at the other occupants of the room, hiding her shock with more flair than a Broadway actress. "Good evening. Did you enjoy your meal?"

"Indeed, Celia, you outdid yourself. Each course surpassed the previous one," said Mr Coleville with a wide smile on his friendly round face.

"Thank you, sir." Celia patted her softly coiled hair and smiled shyly, touched by his compliment. She had always found him to be a most genial man; how had he managed to get chained to that awful woman? It was worse than a Greek tragedy.

Mrs Coleville and Esther had obviously lost their manners, as they merely glanced at each other and smiled tight-lipped. Esther gave Celia a sly once-over, clearly resenting her stylish outfit in contrast to Esther's own frumpy costume. Celia refrained from the temptation to stick out her tongue at her adversary.

Lady Benwick fanned herself, observing Mrs Coleville and Esther's sour response to Mr Coleville's compliment.

"Yes, Celia, you were certainly missed at the dinner table. What a simply delightful dinner," said Mrs Coleville in a saccharine, insincere voice.

Clearly making an effort to impress Lady B, thought Celia.

Esther rolled her eyes to heaven. They almost remained there, until she caught the quelling look Lady Benwick threw her way.

"Are you joining us?" Lady Benwick gestured towards the gold and yellow-flecked sofa next to her.

"No ma'am, I think I will retire. It's been a long day." Celia swiftly exited the room, wrinkling her nose distastefully as she passed through the doorway. She was relieved to be rid of the hypocritical Mrs Coleville and her dreadful daughter. It still irked Celia that the snobbish woman had referred to her as Lady Benwick's 'exotic' companion at a social event not so long ago.

Lady Benwick had placed her hand on Celia's arm to still her rising anger, reminding her of where they were and the family's reputation. However, her guardian had swiftly put the overbearing battle axe in her place, reminding her that Celia was in fact her ward and family, not her official companion. It was only now, thinking back, that Celia noticed with new resentment that her guardian had not corrected Mrs Coleville on the 'exotic' part.

How she wished she could have put that woman in her place, but there was a hierarchy and a protocol amongst the upper classes, and she would have brought shame on the family name. After all they had done for her, her conscience would never allow her to do that.

Ironically, the humiliating incident had taken place at an after-dinner party where a famous black singer from America had been performing with the sole purpose of donating part of her fee to the freedman cause in post-slavery America. She had also given a short talk about educational institutions being built and taught at by black people with some help and support from the freedman society, but mostly from the blood, sweat and tears of black Americans and their supporters.

The abominable Mrs Coleville had acted as if she had never seen an articulate coloured person in her life, despite having her fair share of servants from around the British colonies, some of them more educated than her.

The number of people of colour had decreased steadily since the abolition of slavery in British colonies, as fewer people were running to Britain to escape the plantations or accompanying their masters and mistresses as slave servants and then running away. The risk of being recaptured by hired slave catchers or resold at various venues was no longer a concern.

The deregulation process had taken many years, until chattel slavery had been fully extinguished and eventually transformed into an apprenticeship system. This had not been much of an improvement, as many free slaves became stuck on their original plantations. But the former slaves were no longer officially owned by their former masters and were technically free to create their own destiny.

The tens of thousands of black and mixed people in the colonies in the 18th century were now a fraction of what they were, as they mixed into the native British population, especially in London, or emigrated to other countries around the world. Nevertheless, despite the decrease in migration and immigration, there remained a significant presence, especially in the offspring of mixed relationships, Black Jack mariner communities and the migration of workers, servants and students from Africa and all over its diaspora.

Entering her small apartments, Celia plopped down on her sofa and threw a cushion to the floor. She sat there, shaking with tears of anger and shock. The last time she had felt like this was when her parents had died in a traffic accident when she was merely a child.

In the back of her mind, she had sometimes wondered why Lady Benwick had put up with Mrs Coleville's overbearing demeanour and condescending attitude towards her ward. Celia had thought it was merely the longstanding family connection and the fact that she enjoyed playing bridge with the amiable Mr Coleville.

Well, now the truth had come out. They had been planning an arranged marriage behind her back. *A joining of the families and the fortunes, no doubt,* Celia thought scathingly. How long had this been going on? How could Ed deceive her like this? It was her own fault for eavesdropping; her dear late mother had always told her eavesdroppers never hear good of themselves. Oh, why had not she heeded that advice on this occasion? She wished she could extract the overwhelming devastation building up inside her and throw it at Ed. She would never speak to him again.

Celia fought back tears and bit her bottom lip as she packed some of her toiletries and other smaller belongings into her large leather-trimmed carpet bag—a present from Ed. Jenny, the head housemaid, patted her back in sympathy before leaving Celia to herself. Jenny had been helping her pack her many trunks, ready for the haulage cart to take them away from the townhouse.

She would miss these small apartments...her sanctuary. Celia refused to shed anymore tears over the destruction of Ed's trust and their relationship. The tears that had flowed since she had unwittingly overheard the after-dinner conversation a week ago could fill the famous waterfalls of Jamaica.

Most of her clothes, soft furnishings and other belongings had been transported to the apartments above Georgia's bookshop. Ironically, Lady Benwick had insisted that Celia utilise one of the family's haulage firms and their men.

Georgia, ignorant of Celia's true reasons for making the swift decision to join her in a business partnership and share her apartments, was ecstatic. Celia knew she would have to confide in her soon and reveal her secret. It was a bittersweet arrangement from both sides, as Georgia's sister, Amelia, had emigrated to become a mail order bride somewhere in America's west. Amelia would be sorely missed by both Celia and Georgia.

Lady Benwick had been quite shocked at her decision but had recovered quickly. Strangely, she had been quite willing to accept it without an argument or lecture about the indecency and risks of living as a financially independent, unmarried woman.

"I'm proud of you, my dear," Lady Benwick had proclaimed.

"You don't think I'm being hasty?" Celia asked, surprised at her guardian's agreeable response.

Lady Benwick cocked her head to one side, looking thoughtful. "Possibly. However, I do recall that you've been wrestling with what to do with your inheritance. Whatever guidance I have given and actions I have taken have always been for your own good fortune. But you are of an age where I can no longer feasibly wield my influence over you any longer."

Celia looked at Lady Benwick doubtfully. *Age never stopped her wielding her authority before, so what difference would it make now?*

Lady Benwick ignored Celia's look of disbelief. "It's time for you to spread your wings, my dear. You have been a significant part of our lives since you were a child, and I will certainly miss your daily presence."

"I will always be grateful to you and my godfather for taking me in and treating me as one of the family." Overcome with emotion, she leaned down and kissed the elderly lady on both cheeks.

Lady Benwick's eyes had been suspiciously shiny as she gripped Celia's hands tightly.

To add to Celia's sorrow, she had not spoken to Ed since the incident, despite his many attempts. The betrayal had been too much to contemplate and had knocked her confidence sideways. Avoiding breakfast, she had taken to eating in her apartments, using the excuse that she was not very hungry. She had also stayed above the bookshop overnight on a couple of occasions.

Thankfully, he had been called away on urgent business, so her attempts to avoid him had been resolved. She had written a note to Ed officially ending the relationship and left it on his bedside table. Thinking back, she supposed it had been rather dramatic, but she was deeply irked by his deceit and had not been in her usual practical mindset at all in the last few days.

I heard everything I needed to hear. My eyes are open and my spirit broken... The first line of the letter had barely expressed the indescribable emotions and sense of loss that Celia felt to the depth of her bones.

Celia's thoughts were interrupted by a knock on the door. "Come in."

Jenny entered the room in her grey uniform and starched white apron, looking sheepish. Celia and Jenny had become close friends in the last few months and Celia would miss her. Jenny had promised that she would start to attend the literary society, as she had a great love of reading.

"Jenny? Did you forget something?" Celia asked, looking around the room. As far as she could see, all her belongings that Jenny had taken charge of had been packed.

Jenny walked up to Celia and took her hands in hers. They were warm and plump, and Celia could feel the coarse skin on her palms from years of working as a housemaid.

"I have to confess a secret to you," Jenny almost whispered.

"What secret? What on earth is going on? Are you in trouble?" Celia asked, concerned. *Goodness gracious, is she pregnant?* Lady Benwick would not tolerate that in a staff member and would have Jenny's guts for garters if her suspicions were true. She would most likely insist on booking Jenny into their home for wayward women. Both Celia and Lady Benwick were on the board for the charitable concern, along with Mr Henderson.

Jenny took a deep breath. "The mistress set you and Ed up to fail..."

Celia dropped Jenny's hands in shock. "What?"

Had she heard correctly? She stared at Jenny, waiting for the next sentence, the atmosphere between them suddenly full of tension.

"Milady found out that you and Ed had become more than god brother and god sister," Jenny confessed, her face flushing bright red.

"But...how?"

"I don't know. She wouldn't tell me." Jenny shook her head in disgust. "I'm so ashamed, miss."

"Don't call me that. How many times must I insist on you calling me Celia? Especially now I'm leaving," Celia scolded, but it was habitual; she was more concerned with Jenny's revelation. "How on earth did she find out?" Celia wondered aloud.

Jenny shook her head again.

"Well, well. So that's why she was so eager to arrange a marriage between Ed and Esther," Celia huffed.

"Esther?" Jenny looked horrified. "That woman is a right snob. I swear I never knew anything about that, miss—I mean Celia. Milady threatened to dismiss me if I didn't go along with her despicable scheme. You know my mother is recovering from a serious chest infection and I couldn't afford to lose this job, ma'am." Jenny wrung her hands anxiously.

"I'm so confused. Did Ed know that Lady B knew about our relationship?" Celia asked, puzzled and vexed with herself for ignoring Ed's pleas to discuss the matter before he left on his business trip.

"I doubt that he knew," Jenny replied.

Registering what Jenny had said previously for the first time, Celia frowned and narrowed her eyes. "Jenny, what scheme were you talking about?"

Jenny continued to wring her hands nervously. "You're going to hate me, but I had no choice. I couldn't afford to lose this job as I needed to provide medicine for my mother. You know she's been sick for a long time."

"Yes, of course. Is she not getting better now? Is the compress recipe I gave you not working?" Celia asked, concerned.

Jenny smiled at Celia's ability to put her concerns for her mother over her own confusion and distress. But then Jenny's smile disappeared, and she looked down at the boldly patterned rug beneath her feet. "Your 'loving' guardian bribed me into accusing Master Ed of rape. I went to Mr Henderson to report it and asked him to speak to milady on my behalf..." Jenny hesitated.

Celia, shocked to her core, managed to gently lift Jenny's chin with a shaking hand. "Carry on."

"Milady must have then used the accusation as leverage to bribe the master into marrying that dreadful Esther. I don't know what happened thereafter. She would not confide in me. I've been worried sick, as Master Ed has always been wonderful to me."

Celia let go of Jenny's hand and walked over to the window seat, the dizziness in her head making her feel like she was gliding. She sat down slowly. The whole situation felt surreal.

Jenny ran towards her, falling on her knees and grabbing her hands in desperation. "My mother is a widow with my two younger siblings to feed. What could I do, Celia?" she pleaded.

Celia silently stared into the barren room, and the tears she had promised not to shed fell down her cheeks unchecked. And this was supposed to be her family...? *Where do I go from here?*

Chapter Eight

Celia stood in front of the ornate hall mirror, pulled on lace gloves, then lifted the petite handbag sitting on the mahogany half-table. She ruefully regarded her favourite costume, a smart burgundy outfit embellished with sculpted ruffles and black velvet trim on the cuffs and the neck of the jacket. The last time she had worn it, she had been with Ed, visiting Georgia. It had been her first encounter with Nathan since his return. It felt like a lifetime ago.

Moving into the apartments above the bookshop had been a blessed escape from the overwhelming situation brought about by Lady Benwick's mischief. It had certainly been a challenging and deeply depressing transition from feeling secure in her place within their London household to being completely displaced. She no longer felt sure of where she belonged.

Would she ever be able to trust a man again? She shook her head as if she could simply shake off her self-doubt.

Since moving in above the bookshop, she had spent the first few weeks walking around in a surreal daze, struggling to understand Jenny's revelations about Lady Benwick's machinations and shocked to the core by her guardian's and Ed's deceit. Despite his betrayal, she could not help but miss Ed, especially his contagious laughter and wit.

She knew that she would need to bring up the rape accusation with Mr Henderson, Daniel to her, but she had been too embarrassed to bring up the delicate subject. Women could not simply bring it up in the presence of other women, let alone a man, even if he were a man of the cloth and had probably heard any number of horror stories in the communities that he served.

She had made Jenny promise not to let Lady Benwick know that she had exposed her until Celia had spoken to her. At this point, there was nothing to gain in jeopardising Jenny's position as head housemaid and acting lady's maid for Lady Benwick. The next step should be to speak to Ed, but she just could not bring herself to speak to either of the turncoats she had considered family at the moment.

Surprisingly, Nathan had managed to come to the rescue by distracting both her and Georgia from their inner grievances and turmoil. Georgia was still grappling with her sister's decision to emigrate to America as a mail order bride. Georgia missed Amelia terribly and was quite worried and anxious about the safety of her journey across the Atlantic. They were a right pair at the moment.

Nathan and Georgia had remained in touch over the years and had become great friends. They both had prestigious ancestral and family links to Sierra Leone and so got along famously. Nathan had invited them both to dinner with his Aunt Annette and daughter Elouise. He had also accompanied them to various temperance and other charitable events, as well as the odd coffee house. They had even been to see a coloured American poet raising money for the temperance movement. It had made a refreshing change from moping around the apartments and helped to rebuild their friendship, which had been broken when he had moved to New York and gotten married under duress.

Initially, Celia had attempted to avoid him at all costs, reluctant to have past romantic hurts resurface. She already felt quite silly and used, given Ed's latest antics. But avoiding him was impossible, as he had started attending their weekly literary society. At first, she had been quite distant and turned down his social invitations, but she could hardly ignore his kindness without being incredibly rude, and it would have been quite petty to turn down every invitation.

In fact, she had grown quite fond of his Aunt Annette and his gorgeous daughter, Elouise. She was looking forward to joining his sweet family for an early evening meal today. Quite unorthodox, for little Elouise to be joining their little supper soiree, but that's what she liked about Nathan—he followed the beat of his own drum as much as possible. It was refreshing in this stuffy Victorian society.

Nathan had sent his carriage and driver to collect her and Georgia, but at the last moment there had been some type of crisis with a bookshop order and Georgia had begged off.

The apartments above Georgia's bookshop had a convenient side door and narrow steps leading down to the street door. Pushing away her concerns about the changes in her life over such a short space of time, Celia gave her brown feathered black hat a final imaginary tilt to the side and made her way carefully down the stairway. She stepped out into the broad cobbled alleyway and made her way to Charing Cross Road, walking carefully on the uneven ground in her fashionable black boots with little heels.

Celia stopped abruptly. "What are you doing here?" she asked, confused surprise wrinkling her freckled nose.

Nathan smiled innocently and held out his hand as his Anglo-Indian driver opened the door to the carriage. Celia greeted his driver with a smile and examined Nathan warily as she allowed him to help her up onto the buckboard and into the carriage. On closer inspection, she could see that he was somewhat nervous.

"You look marvellous," Nathan said, admiring her carefully coiffed long hair and smart costume.

"Is something wrong? I thought you were sending the carriage to collect us. By the way, Georgia sends her apologies."

"That's a shame. I'll enlighten you inside the carriage."

Celia glanced suspiciously up into his face. Not wanting to make a scene, she settled herself into the carriage and waited for him to enter. Glancing out of the carriage window, she saw Georgia waving from the window with a big grin on her freckled face. It had always tickled them as children that despite the contrast in their light and dark complexions, they had freckles in common—though Celia's were parked across her nose and Georgia's were sprinkled lightly over the t-zone of her face.

Really, that girl was something else, thought Celia, miffed that she had obviously been set up. She should have known, really. What crisis could you have over a book order that would require you to miss out on a good hearty supper?

Celia sighed and turned to Nathan, who had settled himself on the seat opposite. She regarded him expectantly as he rapped the ceiling with his brass-tipped walking stick to signal to the driver that they were ready. The carriage trundled along the cobbled alleyway into the main street.

"What on earth is going on, Nathan? This is obviously a set-up between you and that Cheshire cat up there."

Celia jerked her head in the direction of Georgia, who was still grinning and spying on them from the drawing room window.

"We've had a change of plan."

"Really?" Celia asked politely, gritting her teeth and trying hard not to kiss them.

"Mm-hmm," Nathan answered, trying not to laugh at the expression on her face.

"I don't appreciate you and Georgia—" Celia paused in mid-sentence as Nathan handed her two pieces of paper. Narrowing her eyes, she took and examined them.

Smiling gleefully, she looked up at him. "How did you get these?" she exclaimed. "It's been almost impossible to get advance tickets for the circus."

Nathan tapped his nose with the tip of his forefinger and smiled mysteriously. "I have my ways."

Celia laughed heartily, feeling excited. Lady Benwick had not approved of attending the circus. So, it would be her first time. "Oh, thank you so much, Nathan. I can't wait." *He's so sweet. It's a pity...* She left the thought hanging in the wardrobe of her mind as their eyes met. He had always had the most beautifully compelling eyes— sloe-eyed and chocolate brown in contrast to his copper complexion. Celia glanced away shyly from the intensity of his gaze.

She felt his fingers gently turning her chin to face him. "We need to talk, Celia," Nathan said solemnly, his husky voice sending heat down her spine.

"We do?" Celia squeaked.

Nathan stroked her bottom lip gently with the tip of his thumb for a second. Celia's stomach tightened and her heart flip-flopped at the intimate gesture. *Give me strength. What is this delicious man doing to me? I can't go through this again, can I?*

"Would you say we had very much rekindled our friendship in the last few weeks?" Nathan inquired.

"I suppose so, yes," Celia admitted, somewhat perplexed about where this was going. Her bottom lip was still tingling from the touch of his surprisingly soft thumb. Considering he had spent some time as a petty officer in the navy, she had expected it to feel much rougher. *He must moisturise regularly,* she thought. Unless he chose to walk around with hands looking like a cracked desert plain, he did not have much choice, with melanated skin like theirs.

"I need you in my life, Celia. I need a wife and Elouise needs some siblings to grow up with," Nathan blurted.

Celia gasped, affronted by his clumsy proposal. "Excuse me? Is that it, then? You just want a broodmare and free childcare?" Celia brushed his hand away, frustrated that she was once again on the edge of tears.

Nathan sighed, then took a deep breath. Celia reluctantly let him take her hands into his. "I'm not doing very well, attempting to ask the love of my life to marry me, am I?"

A smile broke out on Celia's face. "Who, moi?"

"Oui," Nathan replied, amused at the beatific look on her face.

Celia's face dropped. "I can't."

"Whyever not?" Nathan's voice was indignant at her quick change of tone and response, and his eyes narrowed in alarm. "We've grown close again and there is no denying that the attraction between us is palpable," he insisted.

"I'm still not over another," Celia confessed. "I don't trust men anymore. I can't. First you let me down, then him."

Nathan looked at Celia, his expression regretful. "I'm sorry for the part I played in how you feel. It's my biggest regret. I know you've kept your heartache mostly to yourself these past few weeks, but are you referring to Langdon?"

Celia nodded miserably.

"Do you still have feelings for him?" Nathan narrowed his eyes again until they were practically slits. Jealousy glinted in their brown depths.

"Yes, I think so. It's confusing. You can't expect me to turn my feelings on and off like a tap."

"Do you have any feelings for me at all?"

Celia nodded warily.

Nathan smiled, relieved at the revelation. "How much affection do you have for me?" he asked mischievously, stroking her hands through her fingerless, ebony lace gloves. Celia stared down at his elegant fingers, mesmerised by their sensual stroking. She was speechless.

"Celia, look at me, please."

Celia obeyed as if she were in a trance. *How long is he going to keep stroking my hands?* She was struggling to concentrate and felt like a cat in heat. It was quite disconcerting.

"The first time I saw you, all those years ago, I knew you were going to be my wife and the mother of my children one day."

Celia caught her breath, her eyes widening in wonder.

"My wife, God rest her soul, knew how I felt about you. I give thanks every day that she understood, as she herself was in love with another man whom she'd been forbidden to marry. She had sought comfort in me. We made the best of an unfortunate situation," Nathan confessed sadly, looking down at their hands. "I still feel guilty about giving in to my physical needs, and the fact that my temptation resulted in you being hurt and my wife's death in childbirth. Nevertheless, I can never feel regret about the wonderful gift of my daughter. Can you understand that?"

"Yes, of course I can," Celia replied in sympathy, touched that he felt comfortable enough to confide in her. She longed to return Nathan's affections, but she did not dare lead him on, not when she was so conflicted about her feelings for him and for Ed.

"I feel as if God has given us another chance at happiness. I know you need time to regain your trust in me and I'll work hard toward earning it, but I want you to think seriously about my proposal. Do you think you can do that?" Nathan asked.

Celia had no time to think of an answer, as his lips landed on her mouth—softly at first, and then more demanding as their tongues collided and swerved around each other. All thought of leading Nathan on vanished as her mind reeled, every part of her anatomy heating up and her heart thumping in her ribcage so wildly it was deafening her. *Could he hear it?*

Between Ed and Nathan, she was beginning to think that she had no self-control. Was she some kind of wanton harlot? Why could she not resist their advances? Georgia would conk her in her forehead, no doubt, if she could read her mind—she felt it was perfectly normal and healthy for a woman to have sensual thoughts and needs. Well, this was obviously the result of her prim Victorian upbringing with Lady Benwick and the protective boarding school they had attended. Somehow

Georgia had missed being affected by the prim and proper etiquette impressed upon them as young girls.

Nathan pulled back reluctantly, not wanting to get too carried away in the plush confines of the carriage. After all, they were in public, and he had always had the utmost respect for Celia's reputation.

Celia breathlessly leaned back against the cushioned seat as the carriage jostled towards their destination. There was no denying the chemistry between them, but could she allow it to flourish, knowing that she still had lingering feelings for another man?

Nathan and Celia sat eating a delicious meal of chana masala and steamed rice in a secluded trellised area of the circus grounds. Nathan had bought their meals from an Indian cook with his own stall amongst the circus's temporary refreshment facilities.

When the friendly man had told them that he had been born in Calcutta and had served as a steward and cook on a privateer ship, Nathan informed him that he had served in the navy, and they had a good-natured chat about sea life.

It was a humid evening, and Nathan wished that etiquette would allow him to take off his jacket, roll up his sleeves, and undo his stiff collar. The smells of freshly cut grass, sticky candy floss, toffee apples and savoury foods mingled in the night air. They listened to the music coming from the carousels and various musicians busking in the small fair that had been set up around the main circus tent.

The clear night sky glittered with stars, which along with the oil lamps set up on the grounds, illuminated the area. Nathan longed to hold Celia's soft, slender hands in his, but he did not wish to be presumptuous in such a public setting. He comforted himself with being pleased at the glow of happiness that radiated from her pretty features. All he wished to do was protect her and make her happy.

"Did you enjoy yourself?" he asked.

"Thoroughly," Celia replied with gusto and a deep sigh. "It was simply magical. My heart near enough failed to beat at the sight of the trapeze artists. And did you see the way that exquisite young girl balanced on her horse? And goodness, when the lion tamer put his head in the lion's mouth! Seriously, I'm surprised I'm still breathing. I'm certain I held my breath through most of it," Celia said gaily, barely pausing for breath.

Nathan laughed heartily. Ignoring his previous instincts, he reached across the wooden table and drew one of her hands towards him, lightly stroking the inside of her wrist with his thumb.

Except for one unfortunate hiccup with a most obnoxious couple, the evening had been a success. A large-chested woman in ill-fitting, frumpy clothing, whom Celia expected to burst out of her tight corset at any moment, had taken umbrage at having to sit next to a coloured couple in the stands within the circus tent. She had been disparaging them in French to her English husband and refused to take her seat. Nathan had stood up for both of them by asking the couple to at least have the manners to disparage them in English. Humiliated, they had both taken their seats with red faces as some of the audience around them had tittered and even clapped in agreement.

Celia smiled at him shyly. Nathan could sense that she felt self-conscious in the public setting, but she did not pull away from his intimate gesture.

"Thank you for a wonderful evening." Celia could not stop smiling coyly. Then, as if realising she may have overstepped the point of decency or her own moral compass, she tried unsuccessfully to fix her expression.

"You're most welcome. It was completely my pleasure." Nathan gave a slight nod and gazed at her seriously, intensely, as if trying to read her very soul. For one moment they were lost in the other's senses, neither one attempting to draw their gaze away. Waves of awareness danced between them, oscillating sensually in their own unique pattern.

Nathan tried not to shift uncomfortably on the wooden bench, lest his attraction to Celia make itself evident, to his embarrassment. He was thankful for the protection of his dark grey frock coat. He wondered what it would be like between the sheets. Would it be more electric than just the wonder of holding hands and gazing at each other? He yearned for the opportunity to explore her voluptuous, lush curves and eventually plunge into the depths of her body with much-needed purpose and release. Preferably on their marriage bed, of course.

It had been a long time since he had been intimate with a woman, due to his responsibilities with Elouise and the guilt that had not left him since his wife had died giving birth. Since Celia had re-entered his life, he had not been able to think about any other woman. It was impossible. He was determined to put aside his impatience, win her back, and rectify the error in judgement he had made when first attempting to court her.

"Good evening, Celia—Nathan."

They were jolted almost violently from their mutual reverie.

Celia gasped at the sight of Ed and Esther standing above them and reluctantly pulled her hand out of Nathan's light clasp.

"Good evening," Nathan replied politely but with none of the usual warmth in his voice. He was unimpressed with the way they had treated his precious Celia and refused to hide it.

Esther remained silent, merely nodding her head regally in his direction whilst deliberately ignoring Celia. *That young lady has a sour and disagreeable disposition,* thought Nathan, struggling unsuccessfully to maintain a neutral expression and hide his distaste. The young lady had the grace to blush at his direct look of disapproval.

Ed addressed Celia. "Would it be possible to have a quick word with you, please?"

Celia looked at Nathan, unsure. "Would you mind?"

"Of course not, my dear," Nathan replied, trying not to grit his teeth at the absolute cheek of this ingrate who had hurt this sweet girl. He longed to give him a piece of his mind and a thoroughly good hiding, conveniently forgetting that he had been the first man to wound Celia's heart. *It's a good thing for Ed that calling out a man for a duel for the slightest hurt or insult has long fallen out of fashion and legality,* Nathan thought.

As Celia rose and walked off with Ed, Nathan gestured politely to Esther to take the seat opposite him. Esther grudgingly took the seat, clearly bristling with resentment before settling her sharp features into a dour expression.

Nathan mentally grimaced and prepared to make polite conversation whilst they both pretended not to watch

Celia and Ed walk to a more secluded area of the circus grounds. He was bitterly disappointed in the end of an enjoyable evening. Their conversation had him worried; there was definitely some type of connection between Celia and Ed, as much as there was a strong sensual chemistry between himself and Celia.

He snuck a discreet look at them. They were clearly arguing fiercely, even though they were speaking quietly. Nathan could easily read Celia's body language, and her face was a picture of anger. Suddenly, he found himself trying not to burst out loud with laughter and bit down on his lip. She was worse than him when she was displeased and struggling to hide her feelings. A poker player she would never make.

Nathan caught Esther's eye as he dragged his eyes away from the arguing couple. They were starting to attract attention from the swarming crowds. He rose and held out his arm to Esther. "I think we should collect our respective partners, don't you?" he said firmly, not really expecting any protest.

Chapter Nine

Celia stood outside the entrance to Lady Benwick's townhouse in Bedford Square. It felt strange looking at the familiar tall, black front door. It was a daunting moment, waiting for one of the staff to open the door, and knowing that this was no longer her home. She would no longer take off her gloves and handbag and leave them on the hallway mirror stand, much to Lady Benwick's irritation. Or be scolded for running up the stairs like a young chit to relax in the familiarity of her cosy apartments.

James opened the door, interrupting Celia's reverie. After greeting each other politely, he led Celia into the ground floor drawing room. "Master Edward will join you soon, ma'am," he said in his slight northern accent.

"Thank you, James. How have you been keeping?" Celia took a seat on a plump leather wingchair.

"Not too bad, miss. Thank you for asking. It mayn't be appropriate to say it, but you've been missed in this house...by *everyone*," James said pointedly, his face a mask of neutrality. His blue eyes twinkled knowingly.

Celia smiled self-consciously. "Oh, bless you, James. The sentiment is mutual. Is Jenny in?" she asked hopefully. It would be good to see her friend.

"I'm afraid not. The mistress sent her out on a few errands. I'll just fetch some refreshments." He inclined his head.

"Thank you. A cup of Earl Grey tea would be lovely," Celia answered as he exited the room.

She was disappointed that she would not get to speak to Jenny. Her light grey cotton blouse felt a little sticky under her smart jacket in the muggy heat, so she took her miniature Japanese fan out of her bag. It was now the beginning of August. Celia sighed as her mind transported her back to the previous night at the circus. *What an acrimonious end to a great evening.*

Ed had led her away to a more secluded area of the grounds, but not too far away from the sour-faced Esther and stern-faced Nathan, neither of whom had been too pleased at their private conversation.

"I see you haven't wasted any time in replacing me," Ed said. There was bitterness in his accusing tone.

"Pardon me? How dare you, Ed. The cheek of it," Celia whispered furiously. Their heads were almost touching as they attempted to prevent anyone nearby from hearing their painful discord. Celia nodded towards Esther. "Unlike that harridan over there, Nathan is a very dear friend."

"I'm sorry," Ed groaned, pushing his hands through his wavy light brown hair. "I've been sick with worry and acting worse than a bear with a sore head. I think everyone at home is thoroughly fed up with me. I know I've acted disgracefully, but you won't let me explain."

"And why would I do that? It's obvious what happened. Why would I allow you to waste any more of my precious time?" Celia hissed, doing her best not to start feeling sorry for him as she looked up at his distressed expression. He looked pale, and he had lost weight. His hair had not been cut in a while—tendrils were starting to catch the edge of his high, stiff collar.

Celia dragged her gaze away and glanced over at Nathan and Esther. Esther was flirting with an embarrassed Nathan, who was doing his best to keep her entertained whilst discreetly spying on Celia and Ed. Celia wondered what she was saying to him. Even Esther was not immune to Nathan's natural charm, chiselled features and wide, chocolate brown eyes. With his copper-toned skin, he favoured one of the many ancient Nubian statues that he loved to talk about at their literary society.

Clearly Esther had no issues with wealthy coloured men, just poor ones and black women, Celia thought peevishly.

"Celia?" Ed pulled her attention away from her observations by gripping one of her hands. "We need to talk, my love."

"I'm not your love anymore, Ed," Celia retorted, pulling her hand away as if she had been burnt. *Why on earth did we have to see these two on such a special evening?* Celia sighed in resignation. "However, I reluctantly agree that we need some type of closure."

"Will you come by the house tomorrow morning?" Ed suggested, looking dejected at her word choice.

Celia nodded, uncomfortable under his sorrowful gaze.

"I am truly sorry, Celia," Ed said.

"I know," Celia said, annoyed at herself for feeling sympathy at his plight. She was the wronged party here. However, she knew Ed—not as well as she had thought, obviously, but she knew deep down that the situation he had gotten caught up in must have unsettled his conscience, as he was usually quite transparent and honest. "You'd better go back to your betrothed."

"She is not my betrothed," Ed protested, outraged and looking dismayed by Celia's response.

"That's not what I've heard," Celia looked up at Ed unhappily, and their eyes met. Celia could see realisation in his eyes. In that moment he knew he had lost her and there was no turning back.

Suddenly Nathan and Esther appeared at their side. They said their goodbyes and went their separate ways.

Nathan had dropped her at home. He had totally understood her need for closure with Ed and appreciated her honesty and willingness to trust him with this turn of events. Hence her presence in the townhouse this morning, with a clear conscience. *Unlike some people*, she thought sadly.

Where on earth is Nathan? Celia thought. "Oops, that must be a sign," Celia said out loud, smiling to herself at the name slip. She had not been waiting long, but she wished Ed would hurry up, as she was impatient to get away from here and move on with her new life as soon as possible.

"Still talking out loud to yourself, Celia? You know that's a sign of old age. You always were a bit of an old soul. Ed won't be long. I sent him out on an errand."

Celia swung her head around as Lady Benwick entered the room and watched in surprise as she walked towards Celia. James came in behind her with the refreshments and rested them on the oval coffee table between the arranged chairs. Lady Benwick sat on her favourite armchair.

"Good morning, ma'am. Shall I be mother?" Celia said as James discreetly exited the room, unable to look Lady Benwick in the face. She was inwardly simmering with resentment and needed to collect herself. Not waiting for an answer, she proceeded to pour out their tea with shaking hands.

"So, you've finally decided to show your face, my girl? Disgraceful behaviour! After all I've done for you," Lady Benwick, remonstrated, dabbing her eyes with her handkerchief.

Celia gritted her teeth, dismayed at Lady Benwick's dishonest histrionics. *Who exactly is she trying to fool? There are no tears that I can see.*

"Lady B, please stop upsetting yourself." Celia resisted rolling her eyes. "Biscuits?"

"No, thank you," Lady Benwick huffed and sniffed impatiently.

"Ma'am, when did you find out that Ed and I were romantically involved?" Celia asked calmly—much more calmly than she felt.

Lady Benwick had just swallowed some tea. Some of it dribbled down her chin as she opened her mouth in shock at the unexpected question. Using the same lace-trimmed handkerchief she had used to wipe her non-existent tears, she quickly wiped the trickle of tea away before it travelled down to her clothing.

Celia was too upset to be amused. *What would polite society say?* Celia thought grimly.

"Yes, Grandmama, why don't you enlighten us. It's time to tell the truth—and please don't for one minute think that you can continue to pull the wool over our eyes. I've spoken to Daniel Henderson."

Celia and Lady Benwick looked towards the door, one curious and the other dismayed, as Ed entered the room and joined them in the seating area.

"Daniel the curate?" Celia asked. She swung her head back around to Lady Benwick.

Lady Benwick knew she had been rumbled and confessed to everything.

"But how could you take this so far, Grandmama? You had to force poor Jenny into making up an accusation of rape," Ed accused, clearly appalled at the lengths his grandmother would go to in order to preserve the family legacy. Apparently, Jenny had confessed her deceit to him and begged him to clear things up with Daniel. "What if Daniel had not been the discreet curate he is? You took a reckless risk."

Lady Benwick bowed her head, unable to look Ed or Celia in the eye. "I was banking on his discretion. He may be many things displeasing in a curate, but being a gossip is not one of them."

"Did you hate me that much, Lady B? I knew you had no deep love for me, but you were kind and I thought you at least were fond of me," Celia said, regarding Lady Benwick with unshed tears welling in her eyes.

Lady Benwick lifted her head and looked at Celia. "No, I do not hate you, my dear. I just love my family and its legacy more than anything in this world. Ed being with you would have been a social disaster. I had political ambitions for him."

How ironic, Celia thought. Nathan himself was well connected and had his own political ambitions, especially in lobbying for the freedom of all the colonies from European empires. He felt strongly that they had jumped from the fire into the pit once slavery had been abolished. Over the past few hundred years, the former slaves, indentured servants and free people of Sierra Leone and other European colonies had been ransacked culturally, psychologically, spiritually and economically. But they had to be savvy in how they strategised as a people.

A prime example of how future plans could go wrong, Nathan had explained, was how Saint Domingue had fared since the famous black general, Toussaint Louverture, and his fellow black abolitionists and allies of other colours had fought for freedom and independence from France. He was well aware of the political and economic traps that could be set by the colonial elites of this world, once freedoms were gained.

"What about my own ambitions. Do they not matter?" Ed asked crossly.

Lady Benwick snorted. "In my day what I wanted did not count. It was all about lineage and family reputation. Nevertheless, I allowed your mother, my precious and only daughter, to marry a quadroon, the ancestor of a former slave. However, that was absolutely necessary, as the fortune he inherited from his aristocratic father saved the family estate from financial ruin."

"But he was white in society's eyes. You could not detect his African ancestry," Celia said, astonished that her guardian had obviously resented the marriage of her godparents to that extent.

"Exactly," Lady Benwick said, triumphant that someone finally understood her stance. "You are undeniably black, despite your father's mixed ancestry, and you were not exactly born with an aristocratic lineage." Lady Benwick ignored Celia's shocked reaction to her reasoning.

Lady Benwick set her delicate china teacup back on the silver tray. "It is one thing to be charitable to my beloved ward, but indeed it is a whole other thing to marry said ward into my family without some type of aristocratic legacy and a racially acceptable form necessary to elevate within polite society."

Lady Benwick observed Ed's discomfort with shrewd eyes. "It may not be important to you as a man. But what about your sister? Charlotte needs a good match, as you will inherit most of the estate. Family reputation, land, continuity is all that matter, not silly love games."

Feeling overwhelmed, Ed walked over to the slightly open window to get some air, his back towards the occupants of the room.

Celia leaned forward in her seat, her eyes narrowed. "I'm confused. You were a strong advocate for the abolition of slavery across the colonies, along with my parents and godparents, as your parents were before you."

"Celia, please. When will you desist in being so naive about the world around you? What has maintaining a family legacy to do with the abolition of slavery? I'm an advocate neither of slavery nor the mixing of the races or classes," Lady Benwick explained impatiently, blinking rapidly. "Am I not human? Am I not allowed my transgressions and complexities?"

Ed and Celia regarded each other across the room, both speechless.

Nathan and Celia sat on an old wooden bench under the drooping branches of an apple tree in Nathan's narrow garden. His rented townhouse was in Cartwright Gardens, an area in Bloomsbury popular with the professional classes, such as military officers, lawyers and men of the cloth.

Nathan himself was the son and heir of a wealthy merchant family from Freetown in Sierra Leone. On his paternal side, Aunt Annette and his father were siblings and the royal descendants of various generations of the monarchy in the ancient kingdom of Songhai, a great trading state of West Africa. Some of their paternal ancestors through marriage, tribal conflicts, and migration had finally settled in Sierra Leone.

Celia and Nathan had just finished a delicious luncheon prepared by Aunt Annette and the housekeeper; Aunt Annette had come to stay with Nathan to help him with her much-loved grand-niece, Elouise. Before the meal he had taken her to his library and office. To Celia's bookworm delight, the tall bookcases displayed a wide variety of books, their spines a patchwork of browns, greens, and blues embossed with titles in gold lettering. Smaller bookcases contained journals, magazines and periodicals written by various coloured authors, the perusal of which had birthed a passionate discussion about the future of the race both in Africa and the diaspora.

Nathan had spoken about his interest in many subjects including global philosophy and African history, and his legal and political aims regarding the progression of the race. His interest in these subjects had been inspired by his Malian tutor back in Sierra Leone, whom he admired greatly. When he had turned 14, his parents had sent him to be privately educated in England against his will. He was also a former law student at University College London, a profession he had decided not to pursue much to his parents' horror. Wanting to leave his pampered lifestyle for a while and discover the world that he had been taught about in his early years, Nathan had bought a commission with the navy and had eventually become a petty officer. In time his parents had become very proud of his accomplishments.

Today Georgia and his Aunt Annette had taken little Louisa for a walk, so they had some rare time alone. Nathan took Celia's hand and studied her slender fingers. "A penny for your thoughts?" It had been two weeks since they had encountered Ed at the circus and Celia had been very subdued and quiet ever since. Nathan had given her plenty of space to marinate in her thoughts, but he was now becoming impatient. He was desperate to know where he stood. How could he risk losing Celia again?

"I'd like to think you're thinking about me and how much you've missed me this past week, as we've both been so busy with our various affairs of business," he said with a mischievous expression, trying his best to lighten her melancholy mood.

Celia smiled widely, looking up at him from beneath her thick black lashes, and fluttering them outrageously.

"If I'd realised you were so conceited, I would never have confessed to missing your company."

Nathan chuckled and before she could respond, he had lifted her effortlessly into his lap. He kissed her deeply and languidly on her lips. She was simply luscious. Celia lightly bit his bottom lip. He caught his breath for a moment and shifted uncomfortably, regretting placing her on his lap, as the evidence of his action was apparent to both of them now. She moved against him sensuously. Nathan wished with all his being that she was already his wife so he could transfer her up to his bedchamber—the middle of the day be damned, he thought with frustration.

Lost for breath, they eventually pulled apart reluctantly. It would not do for the others, especially his young daughter, to catch them in a compromising position. Celia stroked his full bottom lip lightly with one of her thumbs, their eyes locked on the other, unable to look away. Nathan wondered if she could see into his soul. How precious she had become to him. Yet he was so overwhelmed by his feelings that he had no words to tell her.

Eventually Celia managed to drag her gaze away. "We shouldn't get carried away. They'll be back soon."

"Of course." Nathan was not in any type of agreement at all, but it would serve no purpose or example to be caught in a comprising situation by his beloved daughter. "You've been particularly quiet today."

"Yes. I'm sorry. I've not been the best company to you all. I'm afraid it's all been rather too much to bear at times. My mind and my heart are heavy," Celia confessed.

"You do know you can confide in me?" Nathan assured her.

"Can I?" Celia regarded him warily, her eyes full of unshed tears.

"Yes." Nathan wrapped his arms around her and pulled her head into his shoulder.

Propriety forgotten, Celia snuggled her face into his neck and wept with abandon. Nathan kept her safe in his arms until Celia ran out of tears. His nose close to her soft, tightly curled hair, he drew in the fragrance of lemon and rose soap and oils and kissed her lightly on her forehead. He handed her a clean handkerchief from his pocket.

Self-conscious of her vulnerability and a little embarrassed, Celia leaned back a little. "I went to see Ed, the day after the circus."

Nathan raised one of his eyebrows slightly. This was the first he was hearing about this.

Celia gazed up at him with worry etched across her striking features, wrinkling her upturned nose. "I haven't told Georgia either. It's been hard to bear the burden of truth."

Nathan smiled down at her encouragingly, pleased that she felt comfortable speaking to him about her troubles, even before telling Georgia. Was this progress? He certainly hoped so.

Celia relayed to him the particulars of Ed's deceit and Lady Benwick's misdemeanours and devious strategy for derailing their romance, and how the depth and breadth of their betrayal had impacted her life. Nathan listened in fascination. He was disgusted by the web of lies woven by Lady Benwick and the shocking gullibility of Ed.

"How do you feel about Ed now?" Nathan probed and felt Celia's body tense.

"I'm not sure, to be perfectly honest."

Nathan's heart sank. "Surely you wouldn't take him back."

"Of course not," Celia protested, looking scandalised.

Nathan held back the smile tugging at his full lips and tried not to look too pleased at her response. "Why don't you just admit to yourself that you have feelings for both of us?" He examined her face as he waited for her response.

"I can't," Celia whispered hoarsely.

"Why?"

"Because it feels at odds with who I am. It's strange, I can't just switch my feelings on and off. And...my feelings for you are not the same, they're different. I'm unable to articulate how in my mind, which makes it all so confusing."

Nathan sighed and kissed her forehead. "I think I may know how you feel."

Celia stared at him in surprise.

"When I went to New York and first met my wife, I felt conflicted. My feelings for you were still quite raw, and you were always in the forefront of my mind. Admittedly, I was also strongly attracted to her and impressed with the glamour and affluence of the up-and-coming black elite in the San Juan Hill enclave where I resided. It was all so new and exciting. It took getting her with child to realise my feelings were mostly to do with the excitement of the new environment and lust, rather than love."

Nathan glanced away for a moment, distracted by a butterfly flitting amongst the wildflowers in the small garden. "The moment she told me she was having my child I knew I had lost you forever, as my instinct was to do the right thing and marry her. Of course, my uncle's reputation was also at stake, as he is an established doctor in the community, and it would have ruined us as a family if the news had got back to my parents in Sierra Leone.

You became the one that got away in my mind. My only comfort was knowing that she did not love me, but rather a married man she could not have. So, we came to understand each other, and we decided to be friendly and respectful, making the best of an impossible situation. I truly mourned when she died; I felt responsible. I wish she could have known her beautiful daughter."

Celia cupped his face in her hands and kissed him affectionately on his lips. "I'm no longer the one that got away. You're a good man, Nathan, and I appreciate you sharing such a private experience with me. I know I'm not the most open person at times, but I do wish to share more with you. I truly do. Just give me time and I promise we'll get there."

Startled, Nathan felt his chest fill with heat as it swelled with pleasure. He was deeply touched by the sweet, unexpected gesture and words.

"Celia, you know I adore you. My one wish is to look after you and make you feel safe and loved in this cruel world. Let's throw caution to the wind and get married."

Chapter Ten

"So how long are you and Nathan going to send each other to Coventry?" Georgia asked, her husky voice laced with sarcasm.

"What do you mean?" Celia raised one neatly shaped eyebrow, gazing at Georgia innocently in the ethereal light of the lamp-lit parlour.

"You're both avoiding each other as if running from the bubonic plague. It's beyond ridiculous now." Georgia rolled her eyes, clearly not amused by the situation.

"Well, I suppose if someone asked you to marry them and you answered, 'don't be foolish,' they would avoid you too," Celia responded miserably.

Georgia laughed wickedly but regarded her friend sympathetically.

Celia gave her a stern look. "It's not funny, Georgia. It completely took me by surprise and ruined the moment. Oh, why could I have not answered differently?"

Georgia leaned forward in her chair. "Celia, I've seen the way you look at each other. It's obvious that you fell in love the moment you set eyes on him. I was there, remember?"

Shocked, Celia stared at Georgia with her mouth ajar. "I loved Ed. Are you forgetting him?"

Georgia tsk-tsked and waved her hand dismissively, her eyes now glittering with mischief. "As much as I adore Ed, that, my dear, was merely lust and comfort love. If you had confided in me earlier, I could have enlightened you to your folly."

"Comfort love? Pray, tell. What is that?" asked Celia in a chilly voice, gritting her teeth with annoyance.

As usual, Georgia's sharp observations had hit the target and cut deep. Her detection antenna was half the reason Celia tended not to share her deepest thoughts and concerns until she was good and ready. Especially in situations where she clearly was not ready to hear the raw truth.

Georgia continued to twist the knife of truth. "Is it a coincidence that shortly after Nathan's wife gave birth, you finally gave in to Ed's romantic advances? If your love had been anything other than a comforting childhood familiarity with a dose of good old-fashioned lust mixed in, don't you think you would have been able to overcome any obstacles the old harridan put in your way?"

"Maybe." Celia examined her fingers, unable to look her astute friend in the eye.

"Nathan acknowledged his past mistake, supported you patiently whilst you recovered from Ed's betrayal and laid all his cards on the table. Celia, my love, what more do you need for him to prove his love to you? We get very few chances at genuine true love in this life. As women of the race, it is even harder in this society. I hope you don't throw it all away because you are holding on to past errors as an excuse to trust him again. I love you both and I want the best for you." Georgia smiled kindly at her closest friend.

Celia returned Georgia's smile with understanding and sisterly love. They had both been through so much as young girls and women; even Georgia, who had a white father, had not avoided the judgement and disdain directed at coloured people.

"Stop holding back. Let him know how you feel, my dear. You can't afford to lose him again."

The shabby black hansom cab trundled slowly along the cobbled and paved roads. They were not far from Nathan's townhouse in Cartwright Gardens.

Celia had begun to regret taking the cab—the straw on the floor looked in dire need of changing. She couldn't stand omnibuses or trams, though; they made her nervous. Maybe she was irrational, but so many people had been injured or died in accidents getting on or off those contraptions.

She rapped on the ceiling of the cab to signal to the driver to speed up. Instead, the cab stopped abruptly. Celia pulled at the stiff window and stuck her head out of the carriage.

The red-faced driver huffed in annoyance as he leaned down towards her. "Sorry, miss. There seems to be some sort of 'old-up ahead."

"Don't worry yourself. I'll walk."

Celia carefully exited the cab with the driver's help and paid him handsomely. "Can you wait here? I'll send the maid out with a message if I don't need you."

The driver doffed his hat, looking pleased at the additional funds. "Course, miss. Take your time."

Celia walked quickly down the street. Only a few feet from Nathan's residence, a hansom cab lay on its side, not far from a haulage cart parked at an angle, which had lost most of its furniture. Blood was splashed hither and thither amongst the scattered furniture. It was absolute chaos. Sadly, the hansom cab's brown horse, which had obviously seen better days, had not made it; she watched with sympathy as a policeman lay some tarpaulin over it.

As Celia knocked on Nathan's front door, she looked back at the chaos. There was no sign of any injured humans and Celia prayed that there had been no fatalities.

Nathan's housemaid answered the door, wiping a red nose with a large handkerchief and sniffing loudly.

"Whatever's the matter?" asked Celia, startled by the usually smart maid's dishevelled appearance.

"Oh, Miss Celia, Mr Nathan's been in a serious accident. He's been taken to Kings College Hospital. The mistress and little Miss Elouise are with him. Oh, what if he dies!" she wailed.

Celia stared at her in horror, her heart pounding as if it would burst out of her chest. Her stomach clenched with tension. Forgetting her manners and any ladylike decorum, she lifted her skirts and ran like a madwoman back to the hansom cab. Ignoring the surprised look on the driver's face, she instructed him to drive her to the hospital as she climbed into the carriage.

Thankfully, the traffic had not been affected on the other side of the wide road and the cab made its way to the hospital at a steady pace. But the journey felt like an eternity to Celia as she stared blindly out the window, wringing her hands and wondering bitterly why she had been so obstinate. Had she lost Nathan before she could let him know how she felt?

She was jolted out of her reverie as the driver opened the door, having been oblivious to the cab stopping. Concern dulled the driver's kind face as he helped her down the steep cab step.

"Would you like me to wait for you, miss?"

"No, thank you. I don't know how long I'll be or what to...expect..." Celia paused uncertainly, suddenly scared about what she would find now that she had finally arrived. She reached for her purse and paid him the fee he had asked for with a generous tip.

"Much obliged. All the best, miss." The driver doffed his cap.

"Auntie Celia," a small voice cried.

Celia looked up to see Elouise running towards her and noticed Aunt Annette standing anxiously at the entrance. Elouise jumped into Celia's arms. Celia held her tiny body tight, feeling the damp of the child's tears on her neck. They had become close in the last few months. Celia hugged her as if their lives depended on it.

"Papa is sick," Elouise said into Celia's neck, her voice muffled.

Aunt Annette gently lifted her grandniece from Celia's arms, smiling wanly at Celia. Elouise and her grandaunt had the same light, butter pecan complexion and both had Nathan's heartbreakingly sunny smile. "He'll be pleased to see you," she said.

Celia exhaled with relief, only now realising that she had been holding her breath. She was grateful for the reassuring news but looked at Aunt Annette cautiously. "How is he? What happened?"

"Thankfully he is fine, other than a nasty gash on his forehead, a broken leg and hurt pride." Aunt Annette smiled ruefully. "A runaway horse and cart are an unfortunate combination for a hansom cab travelling in the opposite direction. He was on his way to see you." She gently cupped Celia's worried face. "You were made for each other, my dear. Now I need to get this little minx home. She's had a long day."

Celia sat on the visitor's chair beside Nathan's bed, clasping his hand in hers. He had opened his long-lashed eyes at the sound of her rustling skirts, and they had lit up with joy. However, he had said nothing and now examined her gravely as she looked down at his hand in hers, struggling for words, distressed upon seeing the unfortunate injuries he had acquired.

"Yes." She smiled at him mischievously.

"What?"

"Yes, I'd like to be your wife, if you'll still have me."

"Not out of pity." Nathan looked away.

"My love, a very wise woman talked some much-needed sense into me and reminded me how I felt literally the first time I saw you. I was on my way over to your house when—"

"How did you feel when you first saw me?" Nathan asked, his chocolate brown eyes narrowing.

Celia smiled and blinked nervously. "The same as you, my darling. I knew the first time I saw you that you would be the father of my children. Losing you so soon in those circumstances made me distrust my feelings more than distrusting your sincere intentions. I realise that now."

"Come here, please," Nathan demanded softly. She leaned in, and he kissed her ardently on the lips. Reluctantly pulling away for propriety's sake, he said, "I accept your proposal."

"You—" Celia hit him lightly on the arm with her handbag.

"Nurse, I'm being attacked. Help me," Nathan whispered theatrically in a croaky voice.

They laughed conspiratorially, gazing at each other and clasping hands as if they would never let go.

Epilogue: 1985

"So, what happened to Ed?" Audrey asked.

Aunt B closed the leatherbound journal. "Apparently Lady Benwick's shenanigans knew no bounds and she had made up the story about their financial difficulties. She was exposed by the estate manager, who was sick of being coerced into lying to Ed. Other than her granddaughter Charlotte, she had no one else. She became a very lonely old lady.

"Ed eventually met a lovely Canadian heiress on a business trip to Paris, sold the haulage business and moved to Canada. The rest is history, as they say. Celia kept in touch with Ed and his sister Charlotte by correspondence over the years. Charlotte eventually made a good match. So, there were no hard feelings on their parts. The letters are in the box.

"Celia and Nathan went on to open other businesses, including a book-press. They had three children, one of which was my great-grandmother. Jonathan, you descend from Ed's younger sister, Charlotte."

"What an extraordinary story." Jonathan grinned, his hazel eyes crinkling, charmed by the romantic family connection.

"Do you believe in fate?" Audrey asked Jonathan, her big pink and black earrings swinging as she turned to him.

Jonathan stared at her in surprise. "I don't know, I've never really thought about it."

They gazed at each other for a moment, lost in thought at the bizarreness of the situation.

"Hmm..." Aunt B looked at them knowingly.

Drawn out of their imaginations, they turned back to Aunt B.

"I think it's your turn to take care of the family legacy." Aunt B pushed the wooden storage box towards them. "Both of you."

Jonathan slipped his hand over Audrey's slender brown fingers and clutched her hand, smiling broadly.

They both stared at the cherished box in awe. "Aw... Aunt B, this is the best wedding present!"

The End

About the Author

S. N. Clayton was born and brought up in North London. She is a business educator, author, speaker, and avid reader of many genres.

S. N. Clayton has been a big fan of romantic sagas and historical romance fiction since her late mother unknowingly introduced her to Mills & Boon in her early teens by not reading her library books swiftly enough.

In terms of being able to bridge the gap and showcase the multicultural aspect of Britain from an authentic historical perspective, S. N. Clayton's first story in this trilogy *A Shared History,* was quite an exciting and challenging project to take on, especially in terms of research.

S. N. Clayton is in the process of writing the subsequent books in the series, *A Shared Destiny* and *A Shared Promise*, which have proven just as interesting a challenge to research. S. N. Clayton has included a recommended book list to reflect the depth of meticulous historical research required.

S. N. Clayton lives in Greater London. She currently works as a business educator in the commercial area of learning and development and writes part-time.

www.snclayton.com

Twitter: @MicroBizSNC

Further Reading – Book List

- *Staying Power: The History of Black People in Britain* – Peter Fryer
- *How to be a Victorian* – Ruth Goodman
- *Black and British: A Forgotten History* – David Olusoga
- *Black Americans in Victorian Britain* – Jeffrey Green
- *Black Jacks: African American Seamen in the Age of Sail* – W Jeffrey Bolster
- *Black Gotham: A Family History of African Americans in Nineteenth-Century New York City* – Carla L Peterson
- *Before Harlem: The Black Experience in New York City Before World War I* – Marcy S Sacks
- *Classic Jamaican Cooking* – Caroline Sullivan